Originally published in the UK as *Buckle and Squash and the Monstrous Moat-Dragon* by Macmillan Children's Books

BUCKLE AND SQUASH

THE PERILOUS PRINCESS PLOT

SARAH COURTAULD

SQUARE
FISH
Feiwel and Friends
NEW YORK

For Eliza and Beatrice

SQUARE
FISH

An Imprint of Macmillan
175 Fifth Avenue
New York, NY 10010
mackids.com

BUCKLE AND SQUASH: THE PERILOUS PRINCESS PLOT.
Copyright © 2014 by Sarah Courtauld.
All rights reserved. Printed in the United States of America
by R. R. Donnelley & Sons Company, Harrisonburg, Virginia.

Square Fish and the Square Fish logo are trademarks of Macmillan and
are used by Feiwel and Friends under license from Macmillan.

Our books may be purchased in bulk for promotional, educational, or business
use. Please contact your local bookseller or the Macmillan Corporate and
Premium Sales Department at (800) 221-7945 ext. 5442 or by e-mail
at MacmillanSpecialMarkets@macmillan.com.

A CIP catalogue record for this book is available from the British Library

ISBN 978-1-250-05278-0 (paperback)   ISBN 978-1-250-08015-8 (ebook)

Originally published in the UK as *Buckle and Squash and the Monstrous Moat-Dragon*
by Macmillan Children's Books, a division of Macmillan Publishers Limited.

First published in the United States by Feiwel and Friends
First U.S. Edition: 2015
First Square Fish Edition: 2016
Book designed by Anna Booth
Square Fish logo designed by Filomena Tuosto

1 3 5 7 9 10 8 6 4 2

Chapter One

In which there is some mud.

Once upon a time, when the world was full of princes and princesses, knights and damsels, dragons and lady dragons, it was also full of mud.

Squelchy, squishy, gurgling, sticky, stinky, endless, mud-colored mud.

To the two young girls cleaning out their goat pen, it seemed as if there was an infinite supply of mud in the field behind their old tumbledown farm, which was called Old Tumbledown Farm, in their village in the middle of nowhere, which was called The Middle of Nowhere, in a forgotten corner of the kingdom, which was called The Forgotten Corner of the Kingdom, deep in the realm of Squerb.

I said that they were both cleaning out the goat pen, but that wasn't totally true. Eliza was inside the goat pen, shoveling the mud, while her older sister Lavender was *outside* the goat pen "supervising" her (if by "supervising" you mean "reading an enormous book of fairy tales, while wearing a pointy princess hat"). Occasionally, Lavender put the book down and burst into song:

> "Ooh, Prince Charming
> How handsome you are!
> With a steed so shiny
> And your hair so shiny
> And your teeth so shiny
> And your nose so shiny
> Oooooh, Prince Charming . . . you are a prince."

Inside the goat pen, Eliza gritted her teeth.

She was used to the way her sister's songs rhymed "prince" with "prince," "shiny" with "shiny," and "princess" with "bucketful of hens." But that didn't mean she liked it. As Lavender started on the second verse, Eliza stopped shoveling mud and stuck her spade into the ground.

"You know, ever since you got that book of fairy tales," she said, "you've been unbelievably—"

"Princess-like?" said Lavender. "I know! When I learn French, I'm going to sing all my songs *en français*, and then they'll sound even better."

Eliza exchanged a look of despair with Gertrude,

their goat, who was sitting at the other end of the pen, quietly chewing.

Admittedly, Eliza didn't really know what Gertrude was thinking. But she was pretty sure they understood one another.*

Then, for one beautiful moment, Lavender's singing stopped.

You could almost hear the grass growing, the sun shining, and the moles playing Snap underground.

It didn't last.

"A knight!" Lavender cried, looking out across the field. "A knight upon the high road! I may faint!"

Eliza looked up and saw a small, bald man

---

*What *was* Gertrude thinking really? Was she thinking: "I couldn't agree more. Lavender is the worst singer since Sister Margaret released her album *Songs for Phlegmy Voices*?" Or was she thinking: "I am a magical time-traveling goat from outer space and, WOW, do I regret landing here rather than my intended destination in the year 215346B, where goats are worshipped and float around on silver cushions in the sky?"

Or was she just thinking "Yum" because she had just gobbled one of Eliza's socks off the washing line?

We'll never know.

ambling down the path toward them from the direction of their local village, The Middle of Nowhere.

"That's not a knight," said Eliza. "That's Bob."

"It is a knight, riding upon a steed!"

"No, it's Bob. Carrying some post."

"It *is* a knight," Lavender hissed. "I'm going to faint!"

As Bob ambled along the path past Old Tumbledown Farm, he whistled at Eliza and chucked her a scroll. And, true to her word, Lavender sighed and fell to the ground at the sight of him, as if she had just been tapped on the head by a large, invisible spoon.

"Well?" Lavender whispered to Eliza, as she lay sprawled on the grass with her eyes firmly shut. "How would you rate my faint? Out of ten?"

"I thought you had fainted," said Eliza.

"I have!" Lavender hissed back. "I'd just like some feedback, that's all. How was the faint, overall? Out of ten? Maybe a seven? Do you think that yonder knight is in love with me?"

Eliza looked at her sister, and then looked at Bob, who was walking away down the path, scratching his bum.

And she knew the scroll she was holding in her hands was only going to make things worse.

"He's probably in love with me," said Lavender. "I must compose him a poem, telling him how sad I am to reject his love, for I am destined to marry a prince."

Eliza *really* didn't want to give her sister the scroll in her hands. She knew it was only going to encourage her. Perhaps if she just quietly gave it to Gertrude, Gertrude would gobble it up, and Lavender would never—

"What's that? Is it for me?" said Lavender, springing to her feet and plucking the scroll from

Eliza's hands. She broke the seal, and the scroll sprang open.

"Oooh—Prince Rudolph!"

As Eliza had predicted, it was a portrait of a prince. Lavender already had seven in her collection.

"Lavender," said Eliza. "Do you think you could just help me clean out the goat pen? Because after we do that, we need to feed the chickens. And then the pigs. And then we have to cut the grass . . ."

But Lavender had already skipped into the house to stick the prince's portrait to her bedroom wall. She spent the rest of the afternoon there gazing at it and daydreaming about her destiny, which was almost certainly going to feature a handsome prince.

And Eliza spent the rest of the day working in the fields, daydreaming about *her* destiny. *She* wasn't going to fall in love with some boring prince. She was going to battle dragons and giants. She was going to vanquish monsters and travel to distant mountains.

And she was going to solve mysteries like: *Who ate all the food in the pig-pen?*

And: *Is the incredibly haunted forest really incredibly haunted? Or is it just moderately haunted?*

And: *What really happened to Grandpa Joe?*

Ever since that terrible day of calamity, the day which no one ever talked about, the day when Eliza and Lavender's parents had dressed up as trees for

the village festival and been accidentally eaten by a bear, Eliza and Lavender had been looked after by Grandma Maud and Grandpa Joe.

Every day, Grandma Maud fed the pigs and the goat, and then sat in her sitting room, telling people's fortunes, while Grandpa Joe sat next door, where he worked as a tailor, making his warm and sometimes unusual clothes. Until one day, when Grandpa Joe went out to get some milk.

And then he came back with the milk.

And then he went out to get some air.

And then he came back with the air.

And then he went out to get a paper.

And *then* he never came back.

And no one knew what had hap-pened to him, least of all Grandma Maud. Whenever Eliza asked her, she just said, "Oh, who can say? Perhaps he fell into the Chasm of Infinite Darkness, from which no living soul has ever returned. Or

perhaps he just got lost on the way to the shops. I suppose we'll never know."

As Eliza worked, she imagined her way out of The Middle of Nowhere. She imagined slicing the heads off fire-breathing dragons. She imagined bopping wild beasts on the nose and making them cry. She imagined climbing down into the Chasm of Infinite Darkness and finding her grandpa.

And while Eliza imagined, Gertrude spent the rest of the afternoon sitting in her pen, chewing over *her* destiny. And who *knew* what that would involve?

Chapter Two

In which Prince Chlknklkgkfj makes a brief appearance.

That night, the two sisters were tucked up in bed while Grandma Maud read them a soothing bedtime story. Like many of Grandma Maud's bedtime stories, this one began with the fact that someone called William owed her fifteen silver pieces, and ended with every single symptom of the Black Death.

"And from that day on, he was covered in spots," she said serenely. "And then came the lumps. And then his skin started to wither. And then he collapsed. And then his fingers fell off. And then his legs fell off. And then he died." She smiled. "The end. Would you like another story?"

"No thanks, Grandma," said Eliza.

"Wonderful!" said Grandma Maud. "How about *The Tale of the Little Boy and the Very Deep Well*? Or how about *Young Alexandra and the Pirates Who Completely Murdered Her*? Of course there's always *Lamby the Lamb and the Delicious Sunday Lunch* . . ."

"NO THANK YOU, Grandma," said Eliza and Lavender.

"Oh well. Suit yourselves," said Grandma Maud, heaving herself out of the chair and shuffling over to the door. "Goodnight, sleep tight, and don't let the Black Death get you in the night!"

"We won't!"

"Or the Shrinking Lurgy!"

"We won't."

"Or the Incredibly Fatal Hiccups!"

"We WON'T," said Lavender and Eliza.

"Or just the Fatal Hiccups. Of course, there's nothing you can do, if they do come."

She shrugged, bent down to blow out the candle, and shut the door behind her.

"Night, Lavender," yawned Eliza, curling up under her covers.

"Night," said Lavender, leaping out of bed and lighting the candle again.

Lavender gazed up at all her portraits of princes on the wall. There was:

**Prince Fabian
the Bold**

*Prince Arjuna
the Italic*

Prince Alan
the Underlined

Prince Kanye
the Anachronistic

Prince Chlknklkgkfj
the Unpronounceable

Prince Orhan
the Orphan

"Goodnight, **Prince Fabian**," Lavender began.

"Goodnight, *Prince Arjuna* . . ."

"I AM TRYING TO SLEEP," said Eliza.

"Goodnight, <u>Prince Alan</u>."

"Did you hear what I said?"

But Lavender carried on, right through the list.

Prince Olaf
the Simply Fat

Prince Rudolph
the Unusual

"And goodnight to you, Prince Rudolph the Unusual!" Lavender said finally. "I may not be able to see your face, but I still love you."

Eliza sat up in bed. This was too much.

"Lavender?"

"Yes?"

"You do not love him. You don't *know* him! You've never met him! You don't even know what he looks like!" She jumped out of bed. "Nobody does! Look at that picture! He's holding a hawk in front of his face!"

"Well," said Lavender, "it's not *his* fault his mother was married to his uncle, who was also a horse. He is a prince, and one day I'm going to marry a prince. And—"

"Look," said Eliza. "You have to face it. You're never going to be rescued by a prince. We live on a farm. We're just ordinary people. We're not noble ladies. Grandpa didn't even have a coat of arms."

"Yes he did!" said Lavender.

"All right," said Eliza. "He did have a coat of arms. But that was just because his designs were ... a bit ... unusual. I think maybe he was ahead of his time."

"Not *that* coat of arms. *This* one!" Lavender ran over to the very, very dusty wooden box in the corner. It had an old coat of arms painted on it, and you could make out the words "Buckle and Squash" written across it.

"Here we go," said Eliza.

"You *see*," said Lavender. "We come from a noble family. *Bouclay et Squash*!" (Lavender pronounced Buckle "Bouclay.") "That is our family motto. Which clearly refers to the noble family Bouclay, and the Squash, which is, of course, the vegetable of the Royal Family of Squerb."

Eliza folded her arms and frowned. "No it isn't!"

she said. "That's not what Buckle and Squash means! Firstly, you don't even know where that comes from. Secondly, our ancestors were outlaws."

"Outlaws?"

"They stole from the rich and gave to the poor. Their motto was 'Buckle and Squash,' because that was how they fought."

"That makes no sense whatsoever."

"Of course it does. 'Buckle' stands for the buckle of a sword belt, *obviously*. And 'Squash' is a highly advanced fighting technique, where you defeat your enemy by sitting on top of them."

"Well, I think you made up that whole story."

"Well, I think you made up everything about the noble vegetable."

And so the argument went round and round and round until it became quite dizzy and had to sit down. Because the only person who knew where the coat of arms *really* came from was Grandpa Joe, and unfortunately there was no way of asking him.

Or was there?

No.

"Even if you *did* come from a noble family—which you don't," said Eliza. "Even if you *were* right about the coat of arms, which you're not, how would you even meet a prince, anyway? We live in The Middle of Nowhere. And all the princes live thousands of miles away. Look at the map!"

She pointed to the dog-eared *Map of These 'Ere Parts* on the wall.

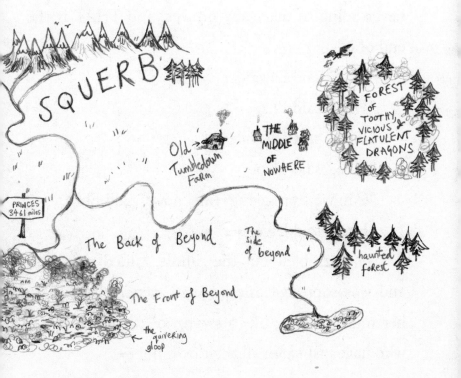

"But we *do* live near the Forest of Dragons!" said Lavender. "And everyone knows that princes love dragon-hunting!"

"But the princes all go hunting in the Forest of Scary-Looking but Surprisingly Sleepy and Stupid Dragons," said Eliza. "We live near the Forest of Toothy, Vicious, and Flatulent Dragons, where no prince in his right mind would ever go! So no more talking about getting rescued by a prince! We're never going to meet any princes, and THAT is the end of it."

"Fine," said Lavender.

"Fine," said Eliza.

"Fine," said Lavender.

"Fine," said Eliza.

"Can we stop saying 'fine' now?" said Eliza.

"Fine," said Lavender.

So Eliza blew out the candle, curled up again, and was soon fast asleep. But Lavender lay awake, her mind buzzing like a swarm of overexcited bees who have just eaten all their own honey.

Because Eliza had given her a brilliant idea.

"The Forest of Toothy, Vicious, and Flatulent Dragons, where no prince *in his right mind* would ever go . . ." she had said. Which meant that a prince *who was not in his right mind* . . . might easily go there!

Very, very quietly, Lavender snuck out of bed, picked up her book of fairy tales and her favorite pointy princess hat, peeled the map off the wall, and tiptoed from the room.

Chapter Three

In which the villain Mordmont is introduced.

Early the next morning:

We would like to apologize for the delay to this chapter, which has been caused by the villain, Mordmont, not doing anything particularly villainous at this time. All he's doing at the moment is eating a slice of cake. He is expected to return to his usual villainy as soon as possible.

ANNOUNCEMENT

We would like to apologize for the further delay to this chapter. Mordmont is now having his post-breakfast nap. He's not really doing anything very villainous at all. Unless you count snoring. And dribbling. Delays to his villainy are expected to continue throughout the day.

Chapter Three Again

In which Mordmont will probably still be snoring. I wouldn't bother reading it if I were you.

"Violet? Violetta! Breakfast time, Violy Wioly!"

Inside the castle, Mordmont was now awake. In fact, he was more than awake, he was up and skipping like a slightly evil hare, through his bedroom, down the stairs, and into his kitchen. He had cake in his stomach, curls in his mustache, and joy in his heart.

Today is going to be a wonderful day, he thought to himself as he flung open the kitchen window and looked out at the moat.

"Breakfast!" he roared as he flung his dragon's breakfast—two Scotch eggs, one Welsh egg, four pieces of ham, and three used handkerchiefs—out through the window and into the moat.

Violet didn't stir. Used handkerchiefs were among her favorite snacks, but she wasn't in a rush to collect her breakfast. She didn't usually listen too hard to what Mordmont had to say. Which wasn't surprising, since she was at least six times taller than him, 34,567 years older, infinitely more intelligent, and didn't particularly appreciate being called "Violy Wioly."

"Hmmmn. No Violy Wioly this morning," Mordmont muttered to himself as he stared down at the still surface of the water, slightly disappointed. "And none of the little Violettas either."

Mordmont sighed. Nothing in the world cheered him up as much as the sight of Violet's bloodstained teeth. He cherished all the sweet things she did for him—like that enormous birthday cake that she'd set fire to and turned into a pile of ashes.

His heart was cheered by the sight of some of her many, many dragon children, tearing around the moat and playing games like "Hide and Seek and Gobble and Crunch."

Bless.

He decided to go outside to see if Violet or the rest of her brood would wake up if he chucked enough stones into the water. But as he got to the front door, he stopped short. His eyes boggled. He gasped. Because the letterbox was stuffed with his least favorite objects in the whole wide world. Bills.

"Bonnet??" he shrieked. "Bonnet??? BONNET! BONNET!!"

Mordmont was pale and quivering like a jelly in an earthquake with a magnitude of at least seven on the Richter scale by the time that Bonnet, his pudding-shaped servant, arrived panting at his side.

"WHAT. ARE. THESE?!" Mordmont gasped, pointing at the bills with a quaking finger.

"They're bills, sire," said Bonnet, stooping to pick them up. As he did so, Mordmont snatched them out of his hands and started to open them.

"One hundred pieces of silver for a stuffed owl? Four hundred pieces of silver for a pair of solid gold shoes? *Six* hundred pieces of silver for a pair of gold shoes for a stuffed owl? Bonnet! WHO has been spending all this money on this USELESS RUBBISH?"

"Um . . ." said Bonnet. He coughed. He never liked giving bad news. "I suppose that would be you, sire."

"That is absurd!" Mordmont said, glancing down at his feet and noticing for the first time that his shoes

Um . . .

were remarkably heavy. And looked, well, definitely . . . quite . . . goldy.

He frowned. "No doubt these were all necessities. And they shall be paid for. Fetch me the chest of silver from the East Wing."

"I, er, I can't," said Bonnet in a small voice.

"Can't?" said Mordmont. "*Can't?*"

"Well, er, the thing is, sire, you lost it, sire. In a bet. Playing poker, sire."

"The *entire* chest of silver?" Mordmont asked.

"No, sire. The East Wing, sire," said Bonnet. "Your friend Lord Tartiflette had it removed this morning."

"Oh," said Mordmont. "I see."

Mordmont paced around the room. He did dimly remember playing poker with his friend Lord Tartiflette.

"So, there's no money left at all?" said Mordmont sadly, slumping to the floor.

"Not exactly, sire," said Bonnet. "Cake, sire?"

Bonnet held out a beautiful porcelain plate, with a large slice of lemon cake on it. Mordmont nodded, and mournfully stuffed it into his mouth.

"I'm a broken man," he said between mouthfuls. "I'm as broken as this plate." He threw the plate across the room and it smashed against the wall. "I don't suppose I won anything at the poker game, did I?"

"Er, only that priceless Chinese plate, sire," said Bonnet.

Mordmont sighed again. He had spent all his

money. He had gambled away half his castle. He wasn't even eating his favorite kind of cake. Life had gone badly wrong, and it was time for some clear thinking.

"I'm a man of simple pleasures," he said. "All I ever wanted was a castle, my own pride of lions, a jeweled crown, a choir of elves singing me awake each morning, sainthood, the power to make gold, the best mustache in Europe, a Jacuzzi, an elephant from the Indies, another one to be its friend, a singing giraffe, the power of invisibility, Magical Cheese Powers, a tiger with the feet of a lamb, the head of a lamb and the body of a lamb— basically, a lamb—power over the sea, power over the letter C . . ."

Dear Reader,

This is just a note to say, I cut the next 4,235 of Mordmont's simple pleasures, because really they weren't that necessary. Or simple. And because I like to save paper where I can.

Love,
Sidney the Tree

"...and a meringue that speaks Japanese," Mordmont said finally. "Is that really too much to ask?"

"Yes! No! Gorilla trousers! What?" Bonnet spluttered as he awoke from a small nap.

"It is clear that I must do a terrible thing," Mordmont went on. A look of pain crossed his face, turned left at his ear, left again, and then crossed back over his face. "I'm going to have to take you to the market and sell you as a slave."

"Yuwhh?" said Bonnet.

"Oh, I know what you're thinking," Mordmont sighed. "How will I cope? Who will make my

33

breakfast cake? Who will sing 'The Loveliest Sheep' to me when I can't sleep? But don't think of me. I'll just have to get by without you."

And Mordmont strode off to brood on the difficulties of his life. Mordmont was fond of brooding. He knew how handsome it made him look.

Unfortunately, as he brooded his way through the hallway, he tripped over a scroll, crashed into a lamp, fell over his own feet . . . and landed sprawled on the floor like a spider, with his nose pressed into that morning's copy of *The Squerb Times*. Inside it was the solution to all his problems.*

"YEAOOOOOW!" Mordmont shrieked as he read the front page. "Bonnet—that's IT! Look!"

He jumped up, bolted back into the kitchen, and

---

*Unfortunately, he didn't read that bit.

thrust the paper into Bonnet's face. "Look! Read! Look!"

So Bonnet read out the headlines:

"*The Black Death: Not As Much Fun As We Thought . . . Women: They're Just Wrong, Says Pope . . . Latest Tonsure Styles for Spring . . .*"

"No—not that. This!" said Mordmont. He snatched the paper back, and read:

> Princess Esmerelda of Vablinsk, kid-napped by notorious villain Deadly Oswold, was returned to her family last night after a ransom of one thousand silver pieces was paid to the deadly criminal.

"That's it!" Mordmont said as he danced a little jig. "Don't you see, Bonnet, don't you see? One princess equals one thousand silver pieces! I don't need to sell you! Besides—how much would you have really fetched anyway? I mean, look at you. The Smallest Giant in the Kingdom. What are you worth, really? A bag of flour? Half a cabbage and a small glass of milk?"

"Thank you for not selling me," said Bonnet quietly.

"Oh, Bonnet, I wasn't really going to sell you. You're basically worthless! All we need to do now is find a princess and kidnap her. Snap her up. Then bingo—Bob's your uncle!"

"But Bob's not my uncle," Bonnet whispered as Mordmont danced around him.

"The ransom will be ours! That is—mine! And then all my troubles will vanish—just like that ridiculous owl!"

And walking over to the windowsill, he picked up a large stuffed owl (which was wearing a pair of gold shoes) and kicked it out of the window.

SPLASH!

"Present for you, Violet!" Mordmont shouted out of the window, although Violet did not reply.

"But . . . how are you going to kidnap a princess?" asked Bonnet.

"Ha!" Mordmont laughed. "I'm not—that would be incredibly hard work, and really far too dangerous. No—you are!"

"I am?" said Bonnet.

"Yes. Not alone, of course. Alone, you couldn't kidnap your own eyebrows. No. You'll just have to find the princess. But you'll need someone's help to catch her. Someone big and strong . . ."

Please don't say Clive, please don't say Clive, please don't say Clive, thought Bonnet.

Of all the things in life Bonnet was scared of (and there were 87,564 at his last count), the thing at the top of the list was . . .

"Clive," said Mordmont.

Chapter Four

In which Gertrude dreams of parsnips.

The next morning was bright and lovely. The birds sang. Dawn rose. Then she went back to bed. Luckily Dawn isn't part of this story. She didn't really get up to that much.

Eliza, however, was up early. She fed the chickens, cut the grass, and washed all her clothes . . . while Lavender lay in bed snoring.

Eliza didn't mind that her sister was fond of staying in bed for hours "practicing being Sleeping Beauty." She didn't *mind* doing all the work on the farm by herself. And if it just so happened that she chopped a few more logs than necessary . . .

. . . that was just a coincidence, and nothing to

do with her sister spending the entire morning in bed. But at lunchtime, when Lavender still hadn't appeared, Eliza decided she'd had enough.

"Lavender. Lavender. Lavender. LAVENDER!" she shouted, standing over her sister's bed. "Are you planning to stay there for a hundred years? Lavender! Lavender?"

And she pulled back the covers, to see the gentle, sleepy face of . . .

"*Gertrude???!* Get out of there! Wait! Then . . . where's Lavender?"

While Gertrude skittered outside, Eliza stomped off to find her sister. She knew all Lavender's favorite spots.

But Lavender wasn't down by the pond, collecting frogs, just in case one of them turned out to be the Frog Prince.

And she wasn't gazing into her mirror, covering her face in flour, so she'd be just as pale as Snow White.

And she wasn't in the kitchen, dressed up as Cinderella, *pretending* to sweep the floor while singing a song.

Lavender had vanished. It was a mystery, even more mysterious than the mystery of Eliza's missing socks.

So Eliza went to ask Grandma Maud if she knew where Lavender had gone.

"Ooh, I expect she's been taken by the Black

Death, dear," said Grandma Maud
as she sat in her rocking chair,
examining a pebble.

"Er, I don't think she has,"
said Eliza with a frown.

"That's the thing with the
Black Death, dear," said
Grandma Maud. "You
never expect it. First you
see the spots. And then the lumps. And then your
skin withers. And then you faint. And then your fingers fall off. And then your legs fall off! And before
you know it—*POOF!* You're gone!"

"I really don't think she's been taken by the Black
Death," said Eliza. "She wasn't even ill."

"Could be the Fatal Hiccups, then," said Grandma
Maud. "When they come, they come lightning
quick."

Eliza sighed. She clearly wasn't going to get any
more sense out of Grandma Maud, so she went and
sat down on her bed and frowned.

Everything's fine, she thought to herself. *Lavender will turn up. It's not as if she's taken the map and run away or anything . . .*

"ARGHHHHHHHH!!!!!!" yelled Eliza, who had sat on one of her sister's hairpins.

"ARGGHHHHHH!" she yelled again, when she looked up and noticed that the *Map of These 'Ere Parts* had vanished.

"Lavender, where HAVE YOU GONE?!"

Chapter Five

In which Bonnet wears a bonnet.

Meanwhile, Bonnet was on his way to kidnap a princess, with Clive.

Clive, who had the shoulders of a bear and the neck of an ox (he kept them in his bag and liked showing them to people sometimes).

Clive, whose favorite hobbies were:

1) Poking Bonnet.
2) Poking Bonnet.
3) Poking Bonnet.
4) ~~Illuminating manuscripts~~ Poking Bonnet.

With his craggy face, his deep gravelly voice, his

spade-shaped head and
his head-shaped spade,
Clive looked like a
violent criminal—which
he was. Bonnet, on the
other hand, was dressed in
a bonnet and a long green
dress, and looked like a
high-born lady—which
he wasn't.

Together they set out on the path to
kidnap the princess. Or rather, Bonnet set out, and
Clive lay back in the cart, chewing bits of straw and
going over the plan.

"So," said Clive. "How do you identify a princess?"

"One," Bonnet wheezed, "she will walk in a
dainty way. Two, she will either be picking flowers or
dancing. Three, she will be wearing a pointy princess
hat. Four, she will almost certainly be singing."

"And when we locate her?"

"I will engage her in ladylike conversation," gasped

Bonnet, a little bit out of breath from dragging the cart, and Clive, along. "I will impersonate a princess."

"And on what topics will you converse with the said princess?"

"Princessy topics," wheezed Bonnet.

"And what would they be?"

"Measles and France," said Bonnet.

"Excellent," said Clive. He knew a lot about ladies, having had a lot of girlfriends,* and he was pretty sure that that's what they liked talking about.

"Now. Just tell me again, one more time. Just to be sure?"

So, between wheezes, Bonnet told him all over again.

"Sorry, Bonnet, I was just listening to a chaffinch," said Clive. "Just tell me again?"

And so Bonnet told him the plan again. He *knew* that Clive knew what the plan was. He knew Clive just enjoyed seeing him drag the cart, and not trip

---

*If by "a lot" you mean "zero."

over his dress, and talk, all at the same time. But he did it anyway, gritting his teeth.

And, in the back of the cart, Clive gritted his teeth too.

(How else do you think he got that deep, gravelly voice?)

All day they roamed across the countryside. They searched high and low, and at medium height, and they only stopped once, for a quick nap at lunchtime. And nothing much happened while they were asleep.

But they didn't find a single princess. Finally, as

the sun was setting, Clive looked around and noticed that the cart was no longer on a road.

"Bonnet," he said. "Where are we?"

"Er . . . Quite near The Middle of Nowhere, I think," said Bonnet.

"The Middle of NOWHERE!"

"Er, I think so. Not far off."

"Well this is *perfect*," Clive roared. "You know what? You really *are* a giant. A GIANT EEJIT! If we have to go back to Mordmont without a princess, he is going to kill me. And after he's killed me, I am going to kill *you*!"

Bonnet nodded. "Let's stick to that order," he said.

"If I see a princess out here, in the middle of no-where, I'll eat my hat, and then I'll eat *your* hat. And then I'll eat Mordmont's hat. That's right, that enormous big furry one, and who knows what that'll do to my digestion—"

"Shhh!" said Bonnet suddenly.

And they both heard it.

The sound of singing. Really terrible singing.

In the next field, a small girl was dancing, picking flowers, wearing a pointy princess hat, and singing:

"Oooh, Prince Rudolph, with your lovely chin (or chins)
They're so very handsome, what do you keep them in (when you're not wearing them)?
I would like to be saved by you and/or him (by which I mean one of the other princes)—

Oooh, Prince Rudolph,
You are . . . a prince."

"That," Lavender said to herself, "will sound wonderful in French.*"

And as she wandered through the field, Bonnet followed behind her on tiptoe. And inside the cart, Clive stood up and tiptoed too, just to be extra quiet.

---

*This has been tested. It doesn't.

Which didn't really work that well, as the cart
itself creaked loudly as it rolled along.

They tiptoed closer and closer and closer.

In front of them, the princess picked flowers,
and twirled, and sang, and soon arrived at the edge
of a tall, dark, forbidding-looking forest . . .

Chapter Six

In which Eliza gallops on a gleaming
white steed.

Meanwhile Eliza was racing through the countryside to rescue her sister on the back of a gleaming white steed. She was riding like the wind, riding so fast her eyes streamed and—oh, wait. No she wasn't. She wasn't even riding like a light breeze. Because Eliza didn't have a gleaming white steed. What she *did* have was a grumpy brown goat.

"Come on, Gertrude!" she said. "Let's GO!!!"

She was sitting on the back of Gertrude, in Gertrude's pen.

"Mnnnnhrr," shrugged Gertrude.

"Come *on*! Don't you care about Lavender AT ALL? Don't you want to hear her singing ever again?"

At this, Gertrude sat down, rested her head on the ground, and shut her eyes.

"What if she's lost and she never comes back? Just think about that!" Eliza said, and in reply Gertrude started to snore, with the ghost of a smile on her face. It was fair to say that Gertrude didn't always enjoy spending time with Lavender. Only last week, Lavender had decided to put on a play of *Cinderella*, and had made Gertrude and Eliza dress up as the Ugly Sisters.

The week before that, she had dressed Gertrude up as her fairy godmother.

The week before that, she had dressed her up as her "delightful French handmaiden Lucille."

It seemed as if Gertrude was going to need a little bit of persuading. But then Eliza had a brilliant idea. She dashed into the house, and in two minutes she was back with one of Grandpa Joe's old fishing rods and the smelliest sock she could find. As if by magic, Gertrude opened her eyes and leaped to her feet. They were on their way.

So Eliza and Gertrude trotted along through fields, and valleys, and fields, and then more fields, and then some more fields, and then a couple of

fields, and after that some more fields. It was a farm-
ing area. And everywhere they went, Eliza asked:
"Have you seen my sister, Lavender? Sort of annoying? Sings a lot? Wears a pointy hat?"

But everyone said: "No," "No," "No," "No,"
"No," and, "We're a leper colony, run away while
you've still got legs!"

Chapter Seven

In which there really are dragons.

At the edge of the forest, Lavender was smiling. *At last!* she thought to herself. *The Forest of Toothy, Vicious, and Flatulent Dragons!*

She stopped to read the sign:

THIS IS THE FOREST OF TOOTHY,
VICIOUS, AND FLATULENT DRAGONS.
DO NOT ENTER.

And, ten steps behind her, Bonnet and Clive stopped too.

"What if she turns around?" hissed Bonnet, suddenly frightened. "I'm not ready yet! She'll see us!"

"Don't worry," Clive hissed back. "If she turns around, we'll just pretend to be sparrows."

"Oh, OK then."

But Lavender didn't turn around. She started to walk into the forest, and beamed as she read the next sign.

SERIOUSLY. RUN AWAY
BEFORE YOU GET EATEN.

And the next one:

WHO DO YOU THINK
IS WRITING THESE SIGNS?
THE ONLY VEGETARIAN DRAGON
IN THE WHOLE FOREST!

And the next one:

FINE. IGNORE ME.
GET EATEN IF YOU LIKE.

I'LL JUST GET BACK TO
MAKING MY QUILT.

Lavender kept smiling as she walked deep into the dark, gloomy forest. Before long, she had found exactly what she was looking for: a cave. She checked it against the picture in her book of fairy tales. It was perfect.

It had piles of bones strewn around the entrance, and low purring sounds coming from inside it, as if the cave was full of cats—giant cats who had giant claws and who smoked a hundred cigarettes a day.

So she tied herself to a nearby rock, placed some assorted meats on the ground next to her, and decided to wait patiently until she was attacked by a dragon—because then she knew she would be rescued by a prince.

As she waited, she read another fairy tale, which reassured her that a handsome prince would be on his way to rescue her very shortly. Soon, she was so excited that she started to sing.

"I can't wait to be rescued by a prince,
If he is bonkers, I won't mind!
If he's a prince he will be kind
And handsome and lovely
And handsome and good
He'll have arms and legs,
Just as he should,
And ankles and feet,
And he won't be made of wood . . .
He will be a PRINCE!"

Inside that dark, mysterious cave, a dragon pricked up her ears.

In fact, there was more than one dragon inside

the cave. There was a mother dragon and, snoozing on her head, was a baby dragon. Here they are:

How sweet, you might think. But then you'd be an idiot.

BECAUSE THEY WERE DRAGONS.

After three weeks of her child's fire-breathing tantrums, the mother dragon had *just* managed to get her baby to sleep. *Peace. Finally, a moment of peace,* she thought. It had been a long three weeks. When her baby dragon cried, his flaming tears set fire to things. When he sneezed, his flaming snot set fire to things. When he was sick, his flaming vomit set fire to things. And by "things," I mean "his mother."

The only time that the baby dragon wasn't

setting fire to "things" was when he was asleep. And now, finally, he was. *Peace*, the mother dragon thought again. *Lovely, quiet, flatulent peace.* For, apart from the low burble of dragon farts, and the peaceful sound of dragons sharpening their teeth and snacking on the occasional traveler, the forest was lovely and quiet.

And then she heard a terrible sound.

Was it a bear sitting on a hedgehog?

Was it an elephant weeping over his math homework?

Was it a rhinoceros being forced to watch *Swan Lake*?

Whatever it was, it had to be stopped. NOW. Before it woke her baby up.

So, as softly as she could, the mother dragon put her baby down, slipped out of the cave, and saw, tied to her favorite rock, a small, strange creature in a tall pointy hat, making the most truly terrible sound that she had ever heard.

⌣⌣⌣

Meanwhile, outside the Forest of Toothy, Vicious, and Flatulent Dragons, Clive was making a slight change to the plan. "I'd love to go into the forest with you, Bonnet. Love to. But I can't."

"Er . . . why not?" asked Bonnet.

"'Llergic to dandelions," said Clive with a shrug.

"Oh," said Bonnet, looking down at Clive's feet, and the large clump of dandelions on the ground beside them. And then looking at the large yellow dandelion in Clive's hat.

"*Forest* dandelions," said Clive. "It's my sinuses. It's a shame, cos I'm very fond of dragons. Some real characters you meet in the dragon world. A lot of my best friends are dragons. Oh well. You run along into the forest—we don't want to lose her."

"Right," said Bonnet weakly. "I'll just . . . go in there . . . on my own . . ."

He looked into the darkness and shuddered.

"Oh, you'll be fine, with your giant strength," said Clive, giving Bonnet a small, friendly clap on the shoulder, which knocked him straight to the ground. After dusting himself off, Bonnet got up again.

"Here I go," said Bonnet. "I mean, what's the worst that could happen?"

"Ooh—getting eaten alive, I'd say," said Clive. "Or maimed. But you'll be fine."

So Bonnet went shuffling off into the mysterious, stinking forest.

"I'm a giant," he muttered quietly to himself. "I am a giant. Quite a small giant. Not a huge giant. But . . . I'm still a giant. I'm a giant. I am a giant. I am a g—"

He stopped short. In the clearing ahead of him,

he could see the princess, who was now tied to a rock. And, in front of the rock, staring down at the princess, with angry yellow eyes and a large, gaping mouth that contained more teeth than the entire collection of Bibbleswick's Tooth Museum, was a VERY, VERY LARGE DRAGON.

Oh, thought Bonnet. *Oh, yes. This is the bit where I rescue the princess from the dragon.* But his mouth was suddenly dry and his feet seemed to be glued to the spot. So he just stood and stared, as Lavender, opening her eyes, came face to snout with the dragon, and the dragon breathed a thick cloud of purple smoke into her face. Here's a closer look at the cloud:

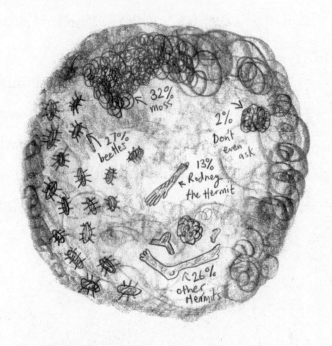

As the smoke cleared, Lavender looked up into two unblinking yellow eyes and she managed to do what she'd been trying to do for so long.

She fainted.

With a grunt, the dragon picked her up by the

tip of her pointy princess hat. She whirled Lavender around in the air, tossed her up and down a couple of times, and shook her a little from side to side. Then she threw her up in the air and caught her by her feet.

I really should do something, Bonnet thought to himself. *I really should. Move, feet, move!* And suddenly, as if by a miracle, his feet did move, and he started to run. Away from the princess, away from the forest, and away from the enormous dragon.

Poached princess? Princess pie? the dragon thought as she whirled Lavender absentmindedly in the air. All of a sudden, the dragon froze, as she heard a familiar sound.

"WAAAARGHHHHHH!"

My baby! Must not wake! Must not cry! No time for cooking! Dashing back into the cave, she tossed the princess and her pointy hat high into the air.

She soared over the trees, just as Bonnet stumbled out of the forest and arrived, panting, at Clive's side.

"I'm sorry," he gasped, "I'm sorry I'm sorry I'm sorry I'm sorry—ooohhhh—duck!"

They both stared with wide-open mouths as the princess came soaring through the sky, and landed with a WHUMPH on the soft straw in the cart.

"Hmmmn," grunted Clive, looking at Bonnet in a whole new light. "Not bad for an oversized dwarf."

Chapter Eight

In which Lavender's dreams
seem to come true.

Lavender opened her eyes and gazed up at the two faces peering down at her.

"My rescuers!" she murmured.

"Yep," said Bonnet, looking at his feet.

"So, which one of you is the prince?" Lavender asked.

Clive cleared his throat.

"We are neither rescuers nor princes," Clive explained. "We are kidnap—"

"RESCUERS!" said Bonnet, elbowing Clive. "We're *rescuers*. That's why . . . we . . . rescued you."

Clive blinked at Bonnet.

"Yes," said Clive. "That's right. My name is Clive, and I am an Organized Criminal and Princess Rescuer."

He decided, since he had met a princess, he had better make some polite, princessy conversation with her.

"So, er, do you have the measles?" he asked.

"Um, I don't think so," said Lavender.

"I'm Clive's assistant," said Bonnet.

"He's a giant," said Clive unhelpfully. "And a lady. He's a lady giant."

At this, Lavender frowned. She couldn't remember quite what happened in this part of the fairy tale, but she was pretty sure it wasn't supposed to go like this.

"I'm not a lady," said Bonnet. "But I am a giant. My parents were giants. I'm just not a very, er, big giant. For a giant."

"I see," said Lavender, who didn't.

"We have rescued you on behalf of the great Prince Mordmont," said Clive. "If you so desire it, we shall accompany you to the prince's castle for your permanent incarceration."

Lavender's head was spinning. Prince? Palace? She didn't exactly know what a "permanent incarceration" was, but she thought it sounded wonderful. Suddenly, everything was beginning to make sense.

"Just one thing," said Clive. "You *are* a princess, aren't you?"

There was a pause.

Then there were some paws. (That was just a nearby rabbit, sniffing around and looking for carrots.)

"Er . . . Yes!" said Lavender.

"Your name?" asked Clive.

"Princess . . . Fahalahalahalaha," said Lavender. And then, because she wasn't sure if her name was impressive enough, she said:

"Princess Fahalahalahalaha Mimsford Lovelynose Cakey McSmith."

"Princess Fahalahalaha Mimsford Lovelynose Cakey McSmith," said Clive. "Of the House of . . . ?"

"Um . . . er . . ."

"Of the House of Ummer! Delighted to meet you. Right you are, Bonnet. Let us now take fair Princess Fahalahalaha—"

"Actually," said Lavender, "it's Fahalahalahalaha, not Fahalahalaha."

"Fahalahalahalaha, not Fahalahalaha," Bonnet repeated.

"That's right," said Lavender. "Fahalahalahalaha, not Fahalahalaha."

"Well then, fair princess . . . fair princess," Clive said. "Let us set off at once for Mordmont's most luxurious and inescapable abode. Full steam ahead!"

So they all trundled off through the countryside.

⌣⌣⌣

As they traveled, Lavender burst into ~~a thousand pieces~~ song. All her dreams had come true! She just couldn't help it. She sang song after song after song. Songs about her prince, songs about the forest, songs about her rescuers, songs about lasagna. And as she sang, it was as if nature responded to her voice. Some nearby squirrels became unexpectedly depressed. Badgers started hitting each other over the head with rocks in order to make themselves deaf. And a whole swarm of wasps became incredibly angry and took out all their rage on some perfectly innocent strangers.

And every once in a while, when Lavender wasn't looking, Clive nailed a piece of parchment to a tree, which read:

THE INCREDIBLY ANNOYING, CONSTANTLY SINGING PRINCESS FAHALAHALAHALAHA OF THE HOUSE OF UMMER HAS BEEN KIDNAPED. SHE WILL ONLY BE RELEESED IF ONE THOUSAND SILVER PIECES ARE SENT TO: MORDMONT'S CASTLE, THE VAGARIES, OX5 FGL.

PS. THE PRINCESS IS BEING HELD IN
A SECRET LOCATION. DEFINITELY
NOT AT: MORDMONT'S CASTLE, THE
VAGARIES, OX5 FGL.

IMPORTANT MESSAGE:

Dear Reader,

The next chapter contains images of violence against trees, which some readers may find upsetting. Particularly if they happen to be trees.

Love,
Sidney the Tree

Chapter Nine

In which there are 3,214 wasps,
all of them called Mildred.

"OW!" screamed Eliza as she got
stung by yet another angry wasp.
It was fair to say that the quest to rescue Lavender was not going well.
Before the wasp attack, she had
already had to counsel several
depressed squirrels.

And she and
Gertrude had
only just
escaped from a badger
battle that involved an entire clan of badgers hurling
rocks at each other . . .

And now this. A cloud of furious wasps swarming madly around her head.

"Come on!" she yelled, and she held on as tightly as she could as Gertrude raced away from the wasps, running so fast that the world around them seemed to blur. Gertrude ran and ran, until the wasps had been left far behind, and when she finally stopped, they found themselves in the middle of a dark and gloomy forest. They were totally lost.

Eliza looked around. There wasn't a soul or a tourist information point in sight. "Hello?" she called, but no one answered. Probably because they were squirrels.

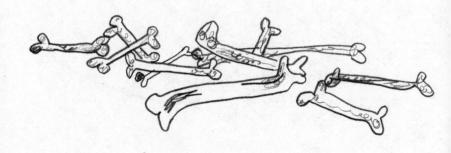

So they walked on, and on and on, through the dark and lonely forest. They walked over ground that was littered with piles of bones, and past caves with eerie, crunching noises coming from inside. They passed a pile of assorted meats, and a rope that looked strangely familiar, but there was no sign of Lavender anywhere. Until they trotted past a sign that read:

THE INCREDIBLY ANNOYING, CONSTANTLY SINGING PRINCESS FAHALAHALAHALAHA OF THE HOUSE OF UMMER HAS BEEN KIDNAPED. SHE WILL ONLY BE RELEESED IF ONE THOUSAND SILVER PIECES ARE SENT TO: MORDMONT'S CASTLE, THE VAGARIES, OX5 FGL.

P.S. THE PRINCESS IS BEING HELD IN A SECRET LOCATION. DEFINITELY NOT AT: MORDMONT'S CASTLE, THE VAGARIES, OX5 FGL.

That is NOT how you spell "kidnapped"! Eliza thought. *Or "released"! Stupid kidnappers, can't they even spell?*

So they trotted on.

"WAIT! Gertrude—reverse!" Eliza yelled.

Gertrude reversed.

Incredibly annoying? Constantly singing?

Eliza frowned at the piece of parchment again.

"LAVENDER! What have you done?" Eliza shouted to no one in particular. "Lavender, you—grrrh!"

And in her frustration, she kicked the nearest tree.

"OW!" said the tree, kicking the nearest squirrel in his frustration.

"OW!" said the squirrel, kicking the nearest snail in his frustration.

"OW!" said the snail, kicking no one at all in his frustration, because he didn't believe in violence.

"Lavender, Lavender, Lavender," Eliza huffed. "First, I am going to find you. Then I am going to rescue you. And then I am going to KILL YOU!"

ANOTHER IMPORTANT MESSAGE:

Dear Reader,

Hello. If you found any of the issues raised in this chapter disturbing, please call our local branch at: 0800-Leaf-Leaf-Leaf. That's my number. I'm always around if you'd like to have a nice chat.

Love,

Sidney the Tree

Chapter Ten

In which there are echoes, echoes, echoes.

As darkness fell, and the wind whistled an annoying tune through the treetops, Eliza and Gertrude trotted valiantly along. They had found an overgrown path, and so they followed it, until they came to a fork in the path, which was confusing. And then they came to a spoon in the path, which was even stranger. And then, just as they passed a ladle in the path, three wizards stepped out in front of them.

"Halt! What do you seek?" they boomed.

In a quavering voice, Eliza told them of her quest to find Mordmont's Castle. And the first wizard replied: "Ooh, that rings a bell. I do know that castle.

It's definitely near here. If it's the one I'm thinking of. Is it, Peter?"

"No, I don't think so. That's the wool shop you're thinking of, Nigel."

"Oh, you're right, Peter. It *is* the wool shop I was thinking of. Sorry, love."

"Thinking of, thinking of, thinking of..." added the third wizard, Frank, who was the wizard in charge of echoes.

"But we can help you on your quest," said Peter. "For we have many weapons in the fight against villainy."

"And all of them are made from wool," added Peter.

"Wool, wool, wool," echoed Frank.

"Yes," said Peter. "We have swords of wool. Shields of wool. Ships of wool. Even horses of wool, such as those that we are riding . . ."

"This is Irene, this is Irene, this is Irene," said Frank, holding out his horse.

". . . and also beards of wool. Umbrellas of wool. Most precious of all, vials of wool, containing magical ointments that heal all wounds."

"Well, they used to, used to, used to," echoed Frank. "But then they sort of leaked, sort of leaked, sort of leaked . . ."

"Silence!" said Peter. "Child, please choose a magical item to help you on your way."

"Er, have you got any gloves?" asked Eliza.

"Gloves! Don't be ridiculous. Gloves made of wool? Whoever heard of such a thing! You may have a hat and a beard."

"Er, all right," said Eliza as he handed her the woolly objects.

"May these aid you on your quest, and never make you itchy. And now we must be on our way. For trials and darkness lie before us, and the wool shop shuts at five o'clock."

"No it doesn't," said Nigel. "It shuts at five thirty."

"Yes, but you know that I like to look at all the different types of wool before I decide what to buy," Peter hissed. "Farewell, young traveler, and good luck."

"Do I have to keep echoing? Do I have to keep echoing? Do I have to keep echoing?" echoed Frank. Then there was a flash, and all three wizards vanished from sight, for they had disguised themselves as leaves floating on the breeze. Except for Frank, who had disguised himself as a bowl of grapefruits.

Chapter Eleven

In which Lavender meets the prince of
her dreams.

That evening, as the sun was setting, and Bonnet
was sweating, the cart rumbled to a stop.

"Princess Fahalahalahalaha," said Clive proudly,
"we have arrived!"

And Lavender looked up to see the castle of her
dreams . . .

. . . and kept looking.

And kept looking.

And looking . . .

Then she tried some gazing . . .

. . . and squinting . . .

But she couldn't see *anything* that looked like the
castle of her dreams. She checked in her book of fairy

tales just to make sure, and she was right. All the castles in her book of fairy tales had tall, elegant turrets and tall, elegant people wandering through their tall, elegant gardens, saying things like:

"Goodness, how elegant and tall we are!"

And: "Thanks, Mama, for giving me Switzerland for Christmas. It's lovely!"

But before her was a green, bubbling moat, and in the middle of it was a gray castle, slumped dangerously to one side, like Grandma Maud when she'd had too much brandy.

"Welcome to Prince Mordmont's Summer Residence!" Clive announced. "And also his Spring Residence, his Autumn Residence, and his Winter Residence."

Lavender gulped.

"Are you sure this is it?" said Lavender, suddenly feeling worried.

"Oh yes," said Clive, putting a large, beefy arm around her.

The castle's rickety drawbridge lowered across

the moat, the portcullis rattled upward, and they crossed over the stinking bubbling water.

"Look out for Violet," said Clive.

"What's that?" said Lavender.

"Violet, the moat-dragon," said Clive. "And her many, many children. There must be—I don't know—a hundred of them swimming around in there. Charming creatures. I'm sure you'll see them when they're hungry."

Lavender looked down into the green water and was pretty sure she saw something moving under the surface. She shuddered. She'd never heard of a prince with his own dragon before, and she'd never heard of a prince's castle that had a bag of rubbish outside the door and smelled a bit like Grandpa Joe's oldest socks, the ones he'd inherited from his great-grandfather.

But there was no time to think, because a moment later they had arrived in the courtyard of the castle, and the front door burst open.

"The prince!" Clive announced.

"The prince!" Lavender gasped.

"The prince!" said the prince, leaping through the door.

Lavender was prepared to be amazed. But . . . Wait! He didn't look anything like the princes in her book of fairy tales. For a start, he wasn't wearing a crown, or long, flowing robes. He wasn't holding a rose, or a slipper. And he didn't have a calm yet gentle face, glowing with a quiet nobility.

No.

This prince was wearing a crumpled pink dressing gown, which seemed to have half a piece of cake stuck to it. He had eyebrows that looked like caterpillars, a long oily mustache, and a beard you could hide an otter in. He was only wearing one shoe. And on his shoeless foot, his toe poked through a hole in his sock, and it was incredibly hairy and also a bit yellow. And instead of processing, or bowing, as princes usually did, he was skipping up and down and clapping his hands.

"You've done it! You've actually done it!" he

shouted. "An actual live princess. A real specimen! This is the happiest day of my life!"

"This," said Clive grandly, "is Princess Fahalahalahalaha. Of the House of Ummer. Princess Fahalahalahalaha, your gracious host, Prince Mordmont."

"Princess Fahalahalahalaha! Enchanted!" said Mordmont. *"Enchanted! Welcome to the family pile!"*

Mordmont pointed to a small pile of pebbles in the middle of the courtyard, as Clive whispered something in his ear.

"Princess Fahalahalahalaha, it is an honor to have you here. Really, this is a quite magical experience for me. Welcome, fair princess. I do hope you enjoy the cell . . . the celebration— which we are holding in your honor in just a few days' time. Now, let me show you to your quarters. It's so wonderful to have a captive . . . audience."

With that, he turned and pranced into the castle. And, not knowing what else she could do, Lavender followed him.

"Mind the puddles!" Mordmont shouted as they walked along a dark, cavernous corridor. "It's just this roof, I'm afraid. These old houses are a real curse. Come along, come along!"

And as Lavender hurried along behind him, Mordmont led her past the ballroom . . .

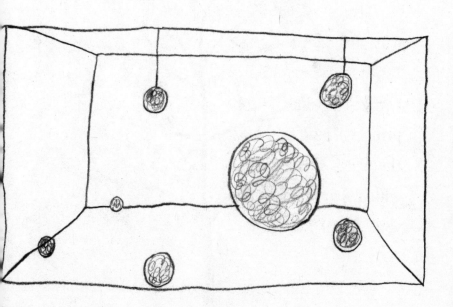

. . . the scullery . . .

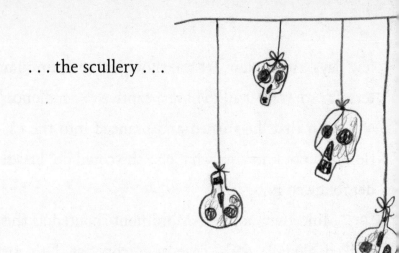

. . . the pantry . . .

. . . and through another gloomy corridor and up a stone spiral staircase. At the top, Lavender stopped and looked at the strange sight in front of her.

Instead of a normal door, the door was barred, like the door to a prison cell. And instead of a bed, there was a pile of straw on the floor, like you might find in a prison cell. In fact, thought Lavender, the whole thing looked very much like . . .

"The guest suite!" said Mordmont. "With en suite bathroom, of course," he said, pointing to a small bucket in the corner.

"But . . . I don't understand," said Lavender, stepping through the door. As soon she stepped into the room, Mordmont slammed the door behind her, plucked a key from his pocket, and turned it in the lock.

"Aha!"

He put his head through the bars, and grinned.

"A ha, ha, ha, ha, ha. Well, Princess Fahalahala-halaha, I do hope you have a very enjoyable kidnapping."

"Kidnapping?" said Lavender.

"Kidnapping."

"*Kidnapping?*"

"Yes, kidnapping!" said Mordmont, who didn't have all day to spend just repeating the word "kidnapping." He had new trousers, and new debts, to get into.

"You have been tricked by my evil plan!" said

Mordmont proudly. "You were brought here under false pretenses. And now you, Princess Fahalahalahalaha, are my prisoner!"

"But, you can't just keep me here!" said Lavender.

"Look, I know I might look beastly to you," Mordmont replied. "But underneath, I'm just a dastardly villain. This is just what I do. When the ransom arrives, you will be free."

"The ransom?"

"One thousand silver pieces. Until it is paid, you will be trapped. As trapped as my wind," said Mordmont grandly, shifting in his breeches. "And like my trapped wind, you will never be free—unless the ransom is paid!"

"I . . . I think there's been a mistake," said Lavender quietly. "I'm afraid you'd better let me go. You see . . ." She gulped. She felt as if she might be sick, and her voice suddenly sounded very, very small. "I'm not . . . I'm not *really* a princess! I was just . . . pretending."

Mordmont looked shocked. "Oh, well then, you must leave immediately," he said in a grave voice before exploding with laughter. "Not a princess? Not a PRINCESS?! Nice try! But I can see your pointy princess hat, and I won't be fooled that easily, Princess Fahalahalahalaha of the House of Ummer."

"But—" said Lavender.

"Oh, don't look so miserable. If this all works out, the ransom will be here any day, and then you can run along home to your castle and do whatever it is you princesses like to do. You can talk about measles and France to your heart's content. And you'll never see this beastly face again!"

And he skipped off back down the stairs, leaving Lavender looking around her cell and shuddering.

Chapter Twelve

In which there is a vision.

"Forests aren't scary," Eliza said to Gertrude as they picked their way through the darkness. "Forests are just trees. And what's scary about trees?"

"Nothing, really," said Sidney the Tree, who they happened to be passing.

"Exactly," said Eliza. "There's nothing to be scared of. And anyway, Lavender's probably fine. Maybe she's been kidnapped by a nice kidnapper who just wants to practice French conversation. Or play cards. Or learn how to faint. Everything's fine. There's no reason to be scared . . ."

"Halt!" said a voice from out of the darkness.

"Er, hello?" said Eliza.

"I am Boris the Wise," said the voice. "I know what you seek, and I can help you."

"You're not another wizard, are you?" said Eliza.

"Certainly not," said the voice as a lantern appeared in the darkness, and Eliza saw a figure crouched next to a large black cauldron. She had a face as wrinkled as a raisin that's been in the bath for a really long time. Like Eliza, she had bright red hair. It sprang out of her head in all directions, as if it was quite embarrassed to be there in the first place, and was trying as hard as it possibly could to leave. As Eliza stepped closer, she deduced that Boris the Wise had not washed in a while, as she smelled a little bit like a stagnant badger.*

"I'm looking for Mordmont's castle," said Eliza.

"I can help you, but my wisdom comes at a price," Boris replied with a crooked smile on her face.

"What do you want?" asked Eliza.

"Only . . . your knees," said Boris.

---

*Eliza was quite wrong about that. Boris had bathed in some pigeon poo only yesterday.

"My knees?"

"Your knees. Just for a day or two. For I am trying to fix my roof, and you should try getting up there with these knees. Do you accept?"

"Um . . . no?"

"Excellent," muttered Boris. "She agrees."

She gazed down into her cauldron, stirring it with a large spoon and mumbling strange words under her breath. Words like "gimbleskimbletilly-tumtickleflub" and "halibut."

Eliza crept closer and gazed into the cauldron too. But all she could see in it was some watery soup and a single, sad-looking turnip.

"I SEE IT NOW!" Boris suddenly shrieked. "THE TURNIP OF DESTINY! HEARKEN! IT WILL COME TO YOUR AID!

DO NOT FORGET!—There, the vision fades. Fades. Fades. Fades . . . It's gone. Ooh—it's coming back! No, that's just an advert. It's gone."

She sighed, and then fixed Eliza with a steely look. "Be gone, child. It is over! Get thee hence!"

But Eliza didn't go anywhere, possibly because she didn't know where "hence" was. She looked down into the cauldron, and then up at Boris again. "Are you quite sure that was the Turnip of Destiny?" she said. "Only I was looking into the cauldron, and the turnip in it . . . Well, it looked just like an ordinary turnip to me. I don't really think you deserve my knees. And you haven't told me where to find Mordmont's castle."

"Child, you know less than nothing! That is the TURNIP OF DINNER. What *I* saw in my vision was the TURNIP OF DESTINY. They are completely different turnips. And if you can't tell the difference between a real turnip and a visionary turnip, that is not my affair. Now, get lost! Go on! Scram! No—not that way! The castle's the other way! That's right. Just over the hill, and then turn left! Be gone!"

So Eliza and Gertrude rode off.

Silly old bat, thought Eliza. *As if she could borrow my knees. What a completely ridiculous idea.*

She looked down at her legs.

"Aaarrrggghhh!"

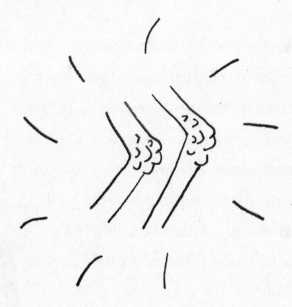

Chapter Thirteen

In which Lavender makes a discovery.

Locked in her cell, Lavender stood and shivered. She stared at the damp pile of straw in the corner, and the spiders' webs hanging from the ceiling, and she felt like the ground beneath her might be about to give way. (And since she was in a badly built castle, on an island floating in the middle of a moat, that might well have been true.)

I'm trapped! she thought. *The ransom is never going to arrive. I'll be locked here until I'm really old ... like, twenty-two ... or even older!*

Since she couldn't bear thinking about it, she curled up on the damp straw bed and opened up her book of fairy tales.

The page fell open on the tale of *Beauty and the Beast*:

Moments earlier, the man in front of her had been a hideous beast. But as she kissed him there was a flash of light. Before her stood the handsome prince she had been dreaming of.

"A wicked fairy put a curse on me," he told her. "She turned me into this hideous beast. Only by finding true love could the curse be broken. Your kiss has broken the spell forever . . ."

Suddenly, everything fell into place. Lavender slammed the book shut, jumped up, and started to pace around the tiny room.

She thought of Mordmont's yellow teeth—teeth

that looked like they belonged to a warthog. And of his wild, wiry eyebrows that looked like they belonged to a warthog. And of his warts, which also looked like they belonged to a warthog.

Of course!

MORDMONT WAS THE BEAST!

Lavender thought of everything he had said to her, from his very first words: "Enchanted! . . . A real curse! . . . Soon, my life will be transformed! . . . This is the happiest day of my life! . . . I might look beastly to you. But underneath, I'm a lovely prince!"*

Mordmont really IS a handsome prince after all! Lavender thought. *He's just trapped by a terrible curse, which has transformed him into a beast and turned his beautiful castle into this hideous ruin!*

And what did her book say could break the spell?

True Love's First Kiss!

That's it, she thought to herself. *Only true love can break the spell! I just need to see Mordmont as the handsome prince he really is. And see this room as the beautiful room it surely is . . .*

That stool in the corner was probably a beautiful dressing table. The pile of straw was a beautiful four-poster bed. That large, hairy spider was probably just an unlucky footman called Graham, trapped by an evil curse.

---

*Mordmont didn't actually say that last bit.

"Poor Graham," Lavender said, and she stroked the spider's hairy back. "Don't worry, Graham, it's all going to be all right," she whispered, before breaking into song:

"Once the spell is broken
My prince will be revealed,
All handsome and kind
and polite and refined
And I'll be wined and dined
I can see in my mind
That he's one of a kind,
In my heart he's enshrined
And our stars are aligned
For our fates are entwined
Now I've found
peace of . . ."

". . . Rind?" said Bonnet, appearing at the door.

"Oh—thank you!" said Lavender, whirling around, her eyes glowing with happiness.

"Rind soup," said Bonnet as he handed her a bowl of thin, gray soup through the bars.

"It looks delicious!" Lavender replied, for she knew that the food was enchanted. If only she could see it as it really was, it would be something like a slice of double dark chocolate fudge cake (with extra chocolate ice cream). It just *looked* like thin, gray soup. But Lavender could imagine how gooey and delicious it looked, and how sweet and delicious it tasted. With all the different layers of chocolatey deliciousness just stacked on top of each other . . .

"This must have taken hours," said Lavender.

"Er, not really," said Bonnet.

"Well, you're very kind."

"Oh, thank you, Your, er, Highness," said Bonnet shyly, his heart melting. (Not literally melting, you understand. That would have been disgusting.) "It was the least I could do," he said with a shrug.

(Which was true. It really was the least he could have done.)

Bonnet trudged off down the stairs, thinking how kind and polite princesses were.

I wish I could help her. But I'm only a tiny giant. What can I do? Bonnet thought to himself, absent-mindedly swinging the keys to Lavender's cell.

Chapter Fourteen

In which Mordmont reveals the secret sweet side that no one knew he had.

Chapter Fifteen

In which there is a kiss.

That night, before Lavender got ready for bed, she decided to practice for True Love's First Kiss by kissing Graham the Footman. He didn't seem to mind, although she did wonder if it would be a bit awkward when the spell was broken, and he became a human and stopped being a spider. Then, just as she was curling up to go to sleep, there came a crash, and a bang, a tumble, and in through the window came . . .

"Eliza?!!!! GERTRUDE! What are you doing here?!"

"Quick!" said Eliza. "Come on! I've come to rescue you!"

"How did you even get up here?"

"Gertrude can climb anything. Now, come on. I think the guard spotted me! Let's go!"

"Eliza," hissed Lavender. "I'm not going anywhere!"

"What?" said Eliza.

"Look, you can't rescue me. I've already been rescued! It's too complicated to explain."

"Come on! We have to go, before someone comes and everything's ruined!" Eliza said.

"No, YOU have to go, before someone comes and everything's ruined!"

"Wait: you don't *want* to be rescued?" said Eliza, her eyes nearly popping out of her head.

"No!" said Lavender. "Of course not! I've found my prince. I'm living in a beautiful castle. Once the spell is broken you'll understand. But if you want me to be happy, you should leave. Right now!"

"I should *leave*?!" said Eliza. "After I got lost in the woods, got attacked by wasps, survived a badger stampede, and climbed all the way up this tower?"

"Exactly!" said Lavender. "That's exactly what I'm saying!"

"Have you completely lost your mind?" Eliza asked.

"No, I have completely found my prince. And if you weren't so jealous, you'd be happy for me. Isn't that right, Graham?"

"Who's Graham?" asked Eliza.

"Graham," Lavender said primly, "is a very nice footman, who has been transformed into a spider by an evil enchantment."

"Right," said Eliza. "You're talking to a spider. And you want me to leave."

"Yes!"

"You don't want to be rescued."

"No! Now go away, before anyone sees."

"Sees what?" said the deep, gravelly voice of Clive, jutting his spade-shaped head through the bars.

"Sea . . . sea . . . *I do like to be beside the seaside*," sang Lavender uncertainly. "I'm just doing my evening singing," she went on as Eliza ducked behind the pile of straw.

"You sure everything's all right in there?" asked Clive. "Thought I heard a bit of a commotion."

"No, no, everything's perfect!" said Lavender.

"Everything's perfect?" said Clive, a little surprised.

"Everything's PERFECT?" said the pile of straw.

"What was that?" asked Clive suspiciously.

"Echoes!" said Lavender. "Funny things. Really, I'm fine in here. Never been better."

"Hmmmmn," said Clive, smelling a rat.

He put the rat back in his pocket. He just liked the smell of them really.

Clive looked around, sighed, and frowned.

"Well, keep a lid on the singing," he growled. "When you're in your own castle, you can sing to your heart's content. But for now, you're Mordmont's prisoner, all right?"

"Of course," said Lavender.

And Clive trundled off back down the stairs.

"Eliza?" said Lavender, waiting for Eliza to come out of her hiding place. "Gertrude?"

But there was no reply.

Chapter Sixteen

In which twenty-three dandelions are eaten.

Meanwhile, with Eliza on her back, Gertrude skittered, hopped, and climbed as delicately as she could down the outside of the tower, which was not very delicately at all, as she lost her footing, fell, and landed on Eliza's head.

OW.

After Eliza's head stopped spinning, she and Gertrude picked themselves up and began to step across the stones that helpfully stretched across the moat.

Hmmmn, thought Eliza as she hopped onto the first stone. *The bump on my head must have confused my brain. I'm sure these stepping stones were in a different place a minute ago. It almost feels like they're moving under us. And they do seem quite spiky, for stones.*

But she kept hopping from one stone to the next as Gertrude reluctantly followed her. Gertrude didn't like water at the best of times. But she particularly didn't like unknown water in the dark. Her hoofs trembled as she jumped across the stones.

Then, just as they were about to step off the last stone and onto the bank, the stone underneath them slid sideways through the water. And opened its eyes.

"Ayyee!" shouted Eliza as quietly as she could, which was not quietly at all. "It's alive! Jump!"

The stepping-stone-with-eyes was now rushing through the moat at quite a pace. Gertrude's eyes were as big as saucers. Her teeth chattered. Her hair stood on end. Eliza leaped, and then Gertrude shut her eyes, and with a terrified bleat she jumped high into the air.

Phew!

They made it by a whisker and landed on the bank in the most elegant manner possible, which was in a tangled heap.

This time, Eliza landed on Gertrude's head. Which sort of evened things out a bit.

"Oh," said Eliza. "Look at that." As she looked back, she noticed that all the stepping stones were moving rapidly through the water. And each one had a pair of brightly glowing, violet eyes.

"Gertrude," she hissed. "I think it might be time to leave."

And she started striding back toward the forest, with the trembling Gertrude running along behind her.

"That is *it*!" said Eliza as they stomped through the forest. "Not only does Lavender *not* allow us to rescue her, she also doesn't warn us at all about the incredibly dangerous creatures in the moat! No 'Oh, you might want to look out because the stepping stones are alive.' No 'Oh, by the way, mind the MONSTERS ON YOUR WAY OUT!'"

"Hrumph," sighed Gertrude, who was still trembling from nose to hoof.

"Well, if she doesn't want to be rescued, she's not going to be rescued!" Eliza said. "That's FINE with me. I don't need to risk my life breaking into castles and escaping monsters! She can just stay in her prison cell and talk to spiders, and I DON'T CARE."

"Hrumph," Gertrude said again, apparently in agreement. But before they got very far, Gertrude stopped. And began to munch on some dandelions.

"Gertrude? Come *on*! We're going home!"

At this, Gertrude sat down. The trip across the moat had terrified her to the bottom of her goaty soul, and she hadn't had as much as a paper bag to eat for hours. When she saw the dandelions, she decided that was it. She wasn't going to move another inch.

"Oh, don't look at me like that!" said Eliza. "Lavender's just going to have to stay there. I'm going home. On my own. I'm going to look after the whole farm, on my own. And I'm going to listen to Grandma Maud's stories about the Black Death ON MY OWN. Come on. Let's go."

Gertrude didn't move.

"Come on!" said Eliza.

These dandelions, Gertrude was discovering, were *much* tastier than the dandelions around Old Tumbledown Farm.

"Well, what am I supposed to do now . . . just stand around waiting for my sister to realize she's trapped?"

"Harrkkkkh," croaked Gertrude.

"Or I suppose I could just find a thousand silver pieces and hand over the ransom?"

"Krrr," Gertrude replied.

"Wait," said Eliza. "So, what you're saying is . . ."

"Chhhhrrrrrrr," rasped Gertrude. (She had a bit of dandelion leaf stuck in her throat.)

"And then, if I . . ."

"Kaaaarrrrrr," said Gertrude. The leaf really was stuck.

"And then I . . ."

"Errrr . . ."

Gertrude was now properly choking, not that Eliza had noticed.

"That's it! I could—just maybe . . ."

"Haaaakkkaaaaaaar!" wheezed Gertrude, toppling over onto her side and slowly turning blue.

"A brilliant plan!"

"Krruuugghhhh!" went Gertrude, desperately trying to breathe.

"I just need a disguise!"

"Yarghhhhhk!" rasped Gertrude, finally coughing up the leaf.

"Yes!" said Eliza. "Gertrude, you are brilliant." She gave Gertrude a friendly pat. "That's *exactly* what I'll do!"

Chapter Seventeen

In which there is giddiness.

The next morning, Lavender was skipping around her tiny cell. Today was THE DAY! She could feel it in her bones. Today they were going to share True Love's First Kiss. She had brushed her hair. She had put on her pointy princess hat. She had dabbed flour on her face and stuck on one of her beauty spots.

She was ready.

When Mordmont strode into the cell, Lavender leaped up to greet him.

"My little prisoner," Mordmont said. "You're looking very . . . happy this morning."

"How could I not be happy?" said Lavender, swaying from side to side. She felt almost giddy with joy. "Soon I hope I will be able to bring you the greatest happiness."

"Very generous of you to see it like that. Of course, my happiness *is* the most important thing," Mordmont replied.

"It is to me," said Lavender. She sighed and gazed at the beast before her. She looked at that horrible mustache, drooping beneath Mordmont's nose like a soggy weasel's tail. And at his yellow teeth . . . and his straggly swamp of a beard . . . and his horrible warts . . . And she thought of the terrible curse that had transformed him into this hideous beast, and her heart went out to him. (Not literally. That would be disgusting.)

"I have one small favor to ask of you," he said.

"Anything," said Lavender.

"Please shut your eyes," said Mordmont.

Shut my eyes? This is the moment! Lavender thought. *The moment I've been waiting for. True Love's First Kiss!*

So she shut her eyes. And waited. And heard a *snip*. And then heard the door clang shut.

When she opened her eyes, the room was empty.

Poor Mordmont. How shy he is! Lavender thought.

And then, looking down, she saw some strands of her hair glinting on the floor and realized what had happened.

He has taken a lock of my hair for safekeeping! How romantic! She sighed.

Meanwhile, Mordmont skipped down the steps feeling very pleased with himself. *Take one lock of her hair,* he thought, *and send it to the House of Ummer as a dreadful warning.* That should get the ransom on its way soon enough.

For the rest of the day, Lavender waited patiently for True Love's First Kiss.

She waited.

And waited.

And waited.

It was evening before Mordmont returned. This time Lavender was sure that he was about to kiss her, because he kept saying romantic things like "When I get my hands on the ransom, I'm going to get some incredible gold trousers," and "I'll be so rich, no woman will be able to resist me," and "I do hope that athlete's foot hasn't come back again."

Lavender smiled at her prince. How shy he was! How sweetly he tried to declare his love for her. In fact, she was pretty sure he was about to kiss her—because now he was picking something long and green out of his teeth—when Bonnet burst into the room, waving a piece of parchment in the air.

"For you, sire!" he said. "It's worked! It's coming!"

Mordmont grabbed it, and feverishly read it out loud:

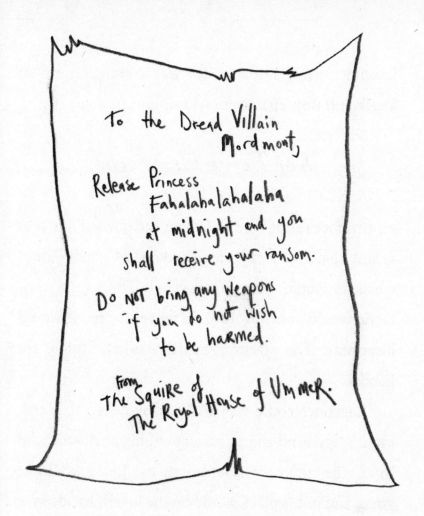

To the Dread Villain Mordmont,

Release Princess Fahalahalahalaha at midnight and you shall receive your ransom.

Do NOT bring any weapons if you do not wish to be harmed.

From The Squire of The Royal House of Ummer.

For a moment, Mordmont froze. Then he leaped into the air.

"It's happening!" he shouted. "It's truly happening! Bonnet, I could kiss you!"

"Please don't, sire," said Bonnet.

"Fine, I'll kiss you instead," he said, turning to

Lavender. And so Lavender was completely taken aback and unprepared for Mordmont to plant . . .

True Love's First Kiss!

on her cheek. But he did. When she opened her eyes again, that haddocky smell would be gone! Those whiskers would have disappeared! The soggy mustache would vanish forever! The yellow teeth would disappear! The swampy beard would be gone for good!

Lavender could feel the cold wetness of Mordmont's lips. And the prickliness of his mustache. But in another moment, Mordmont the Beast would be gone, and in his place would be the lovely, handsome, perfect prince of her dreams.

There was a crash. There was a bang.

That was just Bonnet, tripping over himself as he fell backward down the stairs.

"Don't you just love it when a plan comes

together?" said a voice. "I am going to look so incredible in those gold trousers. Of course, there are bills to pay. But I really do need more trousers. I wonder how many princesses there are in this kingdom?"

Lavender opened her eyes and saw . . .

Mordmont.

With the same horrible mustache and beard.

The same revolting warts.

The same pink dressing gown.

The same unfortunate yellow trousers.

The same unfortunate yellow teeth.

The same haddocky breath.

Mordmont sighed and looked at her.

"It's as if all my dreams have come true!" he said, grinning at her.

"And it's as if mine . . . haven't," said Lavender.

"Well, no, of course not. But I mean, who really cares about you? Not to be rude or anything. But this is the Tale of the Dread Villain Mordmont, and his Rise to Become the Most Dreadful Villain in the

Kingdom.* You're not exactly a significant character.**"

With that, he skipped out of the cell, slamming the door behind him.

Lavender slumped to the floor.

"What a horrible mess," she said, to nobody in particular. "I would really like to go home now, please."

I'm all alone, she thought. And, as if to prove her wrong, Graham the Footman—or, to use his more usual name, "a spider"—crawled all the way up her leg. Which did not make Lavender feel better. At all.

---

*No it isn't.
**Yes she is.

Chapter Eighteen

Which is bathed in a silvery light.

As the clock struck midnight, the moon shone a silvery light over the castle and its surroundings. Clouds raced across the sky, and one of them won and was given a medal. As Mordmont lowered the drawbridge, a dark, shadowy figure appeared at the other end of it, seated on the back of a noble steed.

"He's here," whispered Bonnet. "The squire from the House of Ummer!"

"Greetings, Squire!" Mordmont called into the darkness as he stepped onto the drawbridge, with Lavender by his side. "I am Mordmont! Hand over the ransom, or I'll throw you in the moat and you will be at the mercy of my moat-dragons!"

This was greeted with silence.

"Come on. Be quick about it! Clive, fetch the ransom!"

But as Clive started to pound his way across the drawbridge, the shadowy figure said, "Come no farther! First, the princess must be freed."

"Not until we've seen the silver," Mordmont called back. "Just hand over the ransom, and Bob's your uncle."

"Bob's not my uncle," the squire replied. "He's my third cousin."

Lavender looked into the darkness and wondered who the mysterious figure could be. Was this, perhaps, her true prince?

"The ransom is in this sack," the squire called, holding up a large, bulging sack. "Look!"

The squire flicked a coin through the air, which bounced near Mordmont's feet and plopped into the moat.

"Sorry," called the squire. "I'll just try that again."

A second silver coin came skittering along the drawbridge, and rolled most of the way to Mordmont's feet before it dropped off the edge and into the moat.

"Sorry!" said the squire again. "Listen, I can promise you this—the ransom is genuine. As genuine as my own beard. It is every bit as real as the House of Ummer—on that you have my word."

"What word?" asked Mordmont.

"What?"

"What word?" asked Mordmont again.

"Um . . . 'geranium'?" said the squire.

"I accept," said Mordmont, who was so pleased about getting the ransom he probably would have accepted almost any word, even quite a boring one like "spade."

"Princess Fahalahalahalaha," Mordmont announced, "you are free to go."

So Lavender started to walk across the drawbridge toward the mysterious squire, while the mysterious squire got down from his steed and began to walk toward Lavender, holding out the bulging sack.

Unfortunately, the squire was not to stay shadowy or mysterious for long. For, as he came closer, the wind whistled by and whipped off the squire's beard.

"Yarghhhh!" the squire shouted as the beard, which was made of wool, blew away in a gust of wind.

As the squire reached out to catch it, he dropped the sack, which split and sent silver coins rolling everywhere.

"The ransom!" shrieked Mordmont. "Quick! Bonnet! Clive!"

Mordmont raced after the coins as they went rolling and skipping and flying off the drawbridge in all directions. He picked up as many as he could, stuffing them into his pockets . . . and then suddenly he stopped, and looked at the coin in his hand. All right, it looked silvery, in the silvery light of the moon. But it wasn't, in fact, a coin. It was a pebble.

And so were all the others. His very own pebbles.

"My family pile! You stole my family pile!" Mordmont seethed.

Then, looking up, he gasped.

Lavender gasped too.

Bonnet wheezed.

Clive grunted.

Because, without his beard, the squire wasn't a squire at all.

"You came back!" Lavender shouted to Eliza.

"Came back?!" shrieked Mordmont.

"I'm sorry!" Lavender was shouting. "What do I do?"

Uh-oh, thought Eliza. She hadn't planned this bit. "Run!" she yelled.

So Eliza and Lavender began to run across the drawbridge, toward Gertrude, who was standing on the bank with hope in her eyes and a dandelion in her mouth. But, before they reached the end of the drawbridge, Clive reached the pulley, and the draw-bridge started swinging up into the air.

As Eliza and Lavender scrambled to the edge, they found themselves high above the murky, stink-ing waters of the moat, where strange shapes swirled back and forth below the surface.

"I think this is the bit where we, er . . . jump."

"We jump?" said Lavender. "I can't jump!"

"We have to," said Eliza. "We have to swim for it."

"I can't!" said Lavender. "It's too high."

"Listen, take my hand. One, two, thr—"

But before they could jump anywhere, Clive gave one final tremendous pull on the pulley, and the drawbridge went swinging upward with such force that they were thrown backward through the air.

Whumph! They landed on the ground as the drawbridge shut with a horrible thud.

"Got you!" said a deep, gravelly voice.

And Lavender was once more gazing fuzzily up

into the face of Clive. Except that this time she knew that he was definitely *not* her rescuer.

"What a horrible mess," Lavender said, because she could see that they were now in even more trouble than before. And because she could see all the way up Clive's nose.

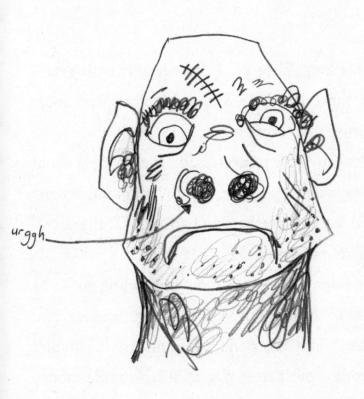

urggh

Chapter Nineteen

In which Graham takes a holiday.

Before long, Eliza and Lavender were sitting back in the cell, which looked gloomier and more frightening than ever.

"Now, my little princesses, don't even *think* about trying to escape this time," said Mordmont, poking his head through the bars and grinning at them.

"We're not princesses," said Eliza.

"And don't *even think* about pretending not to be princesses," Mordmont replied. "Two sisters. Two princesses. Two thousand silver pieces! It couldn't have worked out better. Soon I'll have more money than brains!"

"Soon?" muttered Eliza.

"One little letter to the House of Ummer, and two thousand silver pieces will soon be mine!" Mordmont went on. "Do you have any more sisters?"

"No," said Eliza. "And we're *really* not princesses. We live on a farm—"

"Yes, yes, with a goat called Gertrude—as if anyone would ever believe that," said Mordmont. "But I know that you are Princess Fahalahalahalaha, and Princess—"

"Trahelehelehelehe," said Eliza sarcastically.

"Ha! Caught you off-guard there. Princess Fahalahalahalaha and Princess Trahelehelehelehe, from the House of Ummer. Do you have any brothers?"

"Oh yes. Prince Troholoholoholoho," said Eliza.

"Prince Troholoholoholoho. Very interesting," said Mordmont. "Now, if you're planning to escape, I would just take a moment to consider the lilies. And Violet. Both of which are highly dangerous. Both of which are in the moat."

"Violet?" said Eliza. "The color violet?"

"Violet, my moat-dragon. And all her many

children. I've put her on a strict diet.* So she is ravenously hungry. If you want to try and escape across the moat, go ahead."

And with that, Mordmont was gone. He went tripping down the stairs, thinking about how he was going to spend two thousand pieces of silver. Of course, it didn't need to stop there. *This is only the beginning!* Mordmont thought. *This could be the making of me. I've found my vocation. Kidnapper extraordinaire.* Soon, he was so excited that he began to sing.

"I'll have hundreds of princesses,
Each one will have her nook,
I'll borrow her and give her back
Just like a library book.
And 'happily ever after'
Will live everybodeeeeee
If by everybody you mean . . . me!
And I will kidnap princes,

---

*Mordmont had forgotten to feed her.

And I will kidnap kings,
King Harold, Queen Matilda
And all their diamond rings!
I'll be such a dreadful villain
That no one will resist
And anyone who's anyone
Will want to be . . .
Will queue to be . . .
Will fight until they're blue to be . . .
The very lucky kidnappee
Who's next upon my list."

Sitting on the cold, damp floor of the cell, Lavender and Eliza listened to the echoes of Mordmont's singing, until he finally stopped. (He had been distracted by an incredibly handsome-looking face that he'd spotted in the mirror.)

"Well," said Eliza.

"Well," said Lavender.

"Well," said Eliza.

"Maybe if *I* sang a song . . ." Lavender began.

"Please don't."

"What if I grew my hair, just like Rapunzel, and then let it down out of the window, and—"

"Lavender!" said Eliza.

"What?"

"No more fairy tales," said Eliza with a scowl.

"Sorry," said Lavender. "What if I pretended to be asleep, and then a prince would come and rescue me—"

"LAVENDER," said Eliza.

"Or what if there's a frog in the moat who's really a cursed prince, and he's just waiting for me to dive in and kiss him? I suppose I would have to kiss every frog in the moat, and the toads too, to be safe—"

"LAVENDER!" said Eliza.

"Sorry," said Lavender.

"What did I just say?"

"Er . . . Lavender?" said Lavender.

"NO MORE FAIRY TALES!" said Eliza, and she picked up the book of fairy tales and hurled it out of the window. It landed in the moat with a splash, and was never seen again.

"Eliza!" said Lavender.

"What?" scowled Eliza.

Lavender paused.

"Thanks for trying to rescue me," she said in a very small voice.

"Twice," said Eliza.

"Thanks for coming to rescue me, twice. I'm sorry about everything. It really is all my fault," said Lavender.

"Yep," said Eliza.

"You were just trying to help me."

"*Rescue* you—"

"But I made a mess of everything," said Lavender.

"Yep."

"And now everything's ruined."

"Yep," said Eliza. "Although my plan didn't exactly work either," she added quietly, staring at her fingernails. She hated admitting she was wrong. "I could have had a better disguise. And I suppose I did drop the ransom. I made a mess of everything too."

"Well, you tried," said Lavender, putting an arm around her sister. "At least we're together, that's the most important thing."

"You're right," said Eliza. "That *is* the most important thing."

"This is a bit cheesy," said Bonnet, pushing open the bars to their cell, and setting down two bowls of soup.

"Cheese and turnip soup," he explained.

"Thanks, Bonnet," said Lavender.

"It was the least I could do," said Bonnet. "I hope you are quite comfortable?"

"Not really," said Eliza. "We'd like to go home."

"Of course," said Bonnet. "I only wish there was something I could do to help."

"You could help by giving us the keys," said Eliza.

"The keys?" asked Bonnet innocently.

"Yes, the keys in your hand."

"Oh," Bonnet replied. "Those keys."

For a moment he stood there, his mouth opening and shutting like a slightly confused trout. "Hmmmmmnnnngh," he said. "I'll . . . er . . . I'll . . . yes, I see . . . let me just . . . um . . . yes."

"All you need to do is give them to us," said Eliza, staring at him hard. "It's quite simple."

"You're right," said Bonnet, flushing pink. "Well, here you are."

Bonnet held out his hand.

"Bonnet?" said Eliza.

"Yep?"

"Those aren't the keys. That's a piece of paper, with a picture of some keys on it."

"Is it? Oh. So it is. Er, my mistake. I'll, um . . . I'll . . . just . . . er . . ."

And without finishing his sentence, Bonnet edged backward, locked the cell, and went quickly down the stairs.

I really should help them, Bonnet thought. *They're innocent, after all. And Princess Fahalahalahalaha sings such beautiful songs. Of course I will help them. I must.*

He turned around and started walking back up the stairs.

But then, what about Mordmont?

As Bonnet reached the top step, he came to a halt, turned, and ran back down the stairs again. And he was almost at the bottom of the staircase when another thought popped into his head.

But what will become of the princesses?

So, very slowly, he started tramping back up the stairs again. He was almost at the princesses' cell when a very vivid image popped into his head.

Clive!

Which made him run all the way back down the stairs again.

An hour later, Bonnet was exhausted and dizzy and still holding on to the keys. *What a horrible mess I'm in*, he thought. *But what can I do? I'm only a tiny, cowardly giant.*

And, in an effort to cheer himself up, he decided to go and eat an egg in the bath. He hated being a villain's sidekick's sidekick. It was even worse than his previous jobs, which were:

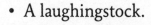

- A laughingstock.
- A human bowling ball.
- Really missing his parents.*
- Crying.*

---

*Those last two weren't really jobs. They were just things he'd done quite a lot of.

Back in the cell, Eliza was trying to force down some of the disgusting soup. It was cold, and as sticky as glue.

"We have to get out of here," said Eliza.

"I know," said Lavender. "Ugh! What happened to your knees?"

"Just . . . don't even ask," said Eliza. She had almost forgotten about her incredibly knobbly old-lady knees. Here they are again, just in case you missed them the first time:

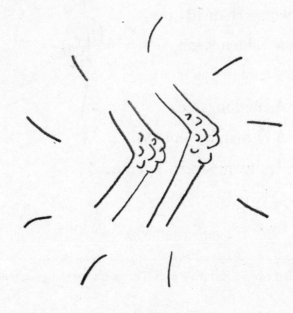

"They're so lumpy and hairy and withered! They're disgusting!"

"I know," said Eliza. "I just had to lend my knees to a witch . . . Oh, never mind."

"You *really* shouldn't have done that," said Lavender unhelpfully. "You don't know what she'll do with them. And those knees won't help us get rescued, will they?"

"Thanks for pointing that out, Lavender," muttered Eliza. "Look, there has to be a way out. I'm sure we can think of something." She shut her eyes tight to help herself think.

And then there was a silence.

It was long.

R e a l l y   l o n g .

It was longer than the world's longest animal. (A Mongolian Death Worm, since you ask.)

"Well?" said Lavender. "Eliza? Eliza, are you *asleep*?"

"Put them in the sheep basket," murmured Eliza.

"Eliza. You *are* asleep!" said Lavender, prodding her sister.

Eliza opened her eyes.

"You're supposed to be working out our escape plan!" said Lavender.

"Sorry," said Eliza. "Let's both think."

So they both thought.

There was another silence, longer than *two* Mongolian Death Worms.

"Maybe we'll think of something in the morning," said Lavender, stifling a yawn.

"Yeah. Maybe," said Eliza.

So they both curled up on the damp straw bed, and shut their eyes, trying not to think about the possibility that they might never escape Mordmont's castle.

"I hope Gertrude's all right," said Eliza.

"I know. And Grandma Maud," Lavender whispered. "She's probably worried sick about us."

In fact, Grandma Maud wasn't doing too badly. Here's what Grandma Maud was doing at that very moment:

"I wonder what she would do if she was here," whispered Lavender.

"She'd tell us a story about the Black Death," Eliza said. "With spots . . ."

"And lumps . . ."

"And withered skin . . ."

"And fingers falling off . . ."

"Wait!" they both said at the same time.

"Are you thinking what I'm thinking?" said Lavender.

"I don't know," said Eliza. "Are you thinking what I'm thinking?"

"I don't know. Let's both say what we're thinking at the same time!"

So they did.

"Let's pretend we've got the Black Death!" said Eliza, at the same time as Lavender said, "Let's sing a song about Grandma Maud!"

Eliza looked down at the gray, gluey cheese and turnip soup, and remembered the words of Boris the Wise. Maybe the turnip could help them after all . . .

Chapter Twenty

In which—Urgh! I wouldn't read this one if
I were you. It's disgusting.

The very next morning, Eliza and Lavender were
awake at the crack of dawn.

"How many stick-on beauty spots have you got?"
whispered Eliza.

"Um . . . seventy-three," said Lavender.

"Seventy-three?!!" said Eliza.

"And a bag of flour to make myself look like
Snow White. It's always good to be prepared."

"And how much sticky soup do we have?"

"Two bowls," said Lavender. "Full of bits of turnip."

"And we've got all these cobwebs . . ."

"Yep," said Lavender.

They took the flour and rubbed it into their skin until they looked as white as ghosts. Then they took Lavender's stick-on beauty spots, and covered themselves with those. They got the cold, gloopy soup and covered their arms and legs with sticky bits of turnip.

Then they took all the spiders' webs from the ceiling and wrapped them around their fingers to make their skin look withered.

"This is the most disgusting thing I have EVER, EVER done," said Lavender. "I do not like this."

"You should try cleaning out Gertrude's pen more often."

"Hmmmmm," said Lavender, frowning. She did not appreciate being made to look disgusting. "If I meet a prince like this, I am going to kill you," she said.

"It's not that likely," said Eliza.

At last they were ready.

"We really are in a horrible mess," Eliza said with a grin.

At about this time, Mordmont sprang out of his bed feeling particularly pleased with himself. "Two thousand silver pieces!" he said. "Two thousand silver pieces! All for ME!"

He danced through the hall, waltzed through the pantry, and skipped up the staircase to check on his prisoners.

"Good mor— Ughhh!" he yelped, looking into the cell. "What is the meaning of this?!" he gasped.

"Oh, it's nothing really. We've just got a few spots," said Lavender in a weak, quavering voice. (Lavender had an amazing sick voice. She had used it many times before to get out of cleaning Gertrude's pen. But it had never had such a dramatic effect as it did now.)

"*Spots?*" said Mordmont.

"Only fifteen or so," said Eliza.

"I've got twenty-three," Lavender croaked proudly. "But then she has got more lumps. Would you like to see them?"

"A thousand times, no," said Mordmont very quickly before he yelped again. "What on earth happened to your knees?! They're so . . . withered!"

"Oh, er, I see what you mean," said Eliza.

Mordmont shuddered and turned to Lavender. "Princess Fahalahalahalaha, why is your hand in a bandage?"

"Oh, it's a bit embarrassing," said Lavender. "I . . . I . . . oh, oh dear . . ."

And then Lavender slumped to one side and

collapsed onto the floor, in her most convincing faint ever.

"What is wrong with her?!" said Mordmont. "What have you done to her! Why has she collapsed? What is going ON?"

"Er, a bit of her finger, sort of . . . fell off . . . in the night," said Eliza apologetically. "She's just feeling a bit peaky."

And Eliza held up what looked a lot like a withered fingertip. (Although on closer inspection it looked a lot more like a withered turnip.)

"Spots," said Mordmont, growing paler by the second. "Lumps . . . Withered skin . . . Collapsing . . . Fingers that fall off . . . That can only mean one thing . . . THE BLACK DEATH!"

And then, as if his mustache had been set on fire, Mordmont started hopping up and down.

"OUT! GET OUT! OUT! OUT! OUT! OUT! GET OUT OF MY CASTLE!"

"Oh, are we free to go?" said Lavender, opening her eyes. "That's very kind of you."

And they both stood up to give Mordmont a grateful hug.

"DON'T TOUCH ME!" he shrieked. "GET AWAY! GET AWAY! GET AWAY! GET AWAY! GO ON GO ON GO ON GO ON—GET OUT GET OUT GET OUT GET OUT!!!"

And he chased them out of the cell, down the stairs, through the pantry, the scullery, the ballroom, the hall, and right out of the front door of the castle.

"BE GONE!!!!" he screeched. And with a last swift, powerful kick, Mordmont sent his horribly diseased prisoners flying through the air, to freedom!

If by the word "freedom" you mean "a stinking, deadly moat, full of monstrous moat-dragons."

Chapter Twenty-One

In which there is something slimy.

"Yaaaaaaaaaaaaaaargh!"

The girls plunged straight into the yellowy-green slime, and were hit by a smell worse than Gertrude's morning breath.

"Gurgggghhhh," said Lavender, surfacing with her eyes shut tight.

"Erghhhhhh," said Eliza, doggy-paddling beside her, squinting, and trying hard not to breathe in the fumes, as tendrils of moat weed wrapped themselves around her arms, and legs, and ankles. They were soft and they were everywhere, wrapping themselves around her like strands of witch's hair.

"Bleurghhhghhh," coughed Lavender as she

accidentally swallowed a mouthful of moat water. It tasted like a seasick goblin's vomit. She pulled her chin as high out of the water as she could, with her eyes still shut, and swam round and round in a circle.

"This way!" Eliza shouted. As they shrieked and swam and splashed and screamed, Bonnet, who was having a quiet nap in the kitchen, woke up and pattered over to the window.

And the moat-dragons, who were also having a quiet nap, deep in the moat, woke up too.

The prisoners! The prisoners have escaped! Bonnet thought. *They're free!* He smiled. And then he remembered the moat-dragons. *Oohhhh! Someone should rescue them. Really. Someone should really rescue them. Now.* Bonnet gulped as he looked out across the moat to the forest beyond. *Perhaps a knight will ride by. Or a prince? A prince on a bright white steed?* But no prince materialized. All Bonnet could see from his window was a slightly sad-looking goat nibbling flowers on the outskirts of the forest. *Hmmmmn.*

"*Ggg*-maybe the moat-dragons are *gg*-asleep!" gurgled Eliza.

But just as she said that, she heard a hissing. And then a snorting, snuffling sound. As Eliza turned her head, she caught sight of several pairs of bright eyes, staring back at her. The eyes glowed violet, and they belonged to three bright green heads, each topped with long, sharp spikes.

"YARGHHHHH!" screamed Eliza.

"ARGHHHH!" screamed Lavender. The two of them started swimming as fast as they could through the thick, treacly water. There's nothing like a horde of ravenous moat-dragons chasing you to make you zoom across a moat at an incredible speed.

Well, there are *some* things. Like magical powers, or a dolphin to ride on, or three wizards suddenly appearing and giving you a ship made of wool to sail away on. Any of those would have been great. Apart from the last one: that probably wouldn't have worked at all. But Lavender and Eliza didn't have anything to help them, apart from their fear. And that gave them a surge of energy and they swam as fast as they could.

As she swam, Lavender thought about the swooshing, rushing, snapping, gnashing sounds that were coming from behind her. They almost certainly weren't from moat-dragons, surging along in the water, getting more and more hungry and excited as they got closer to their prey.

No, she thought. They were probably just the sounds of lilies, floating on the moat. The lilies had probably always made those snapping, toothy, bitey, snarly, hungry sounds, only she had never really listened to them before.

And those sharp jabbing pains in her toes? They definitely weren't moat-dragons biting them because they felt like a cheeky little pre-dinner snack. Definitely not. Those pains were probably just some totally harmless bitey water.

Lavender and Eliza kept swimming, and swimming, with the dragons streaking through the water behind them. The girls' arms felt like lead, and their legs felt like lead, and it was lucky they weren't actually made of lead, because then they would definitely have sunk, or been used to make pipes. But soon they were almost at the bank, and beyond that was the forest. And standing under the trees, not far off, was Gertrude, looking wildly excited to see them after all this time.

"Done it," Eliza gasped, "we've done it!" as they

both reached the bank and pulled themselves up and out of the water. A second slower and the dragons would have had them for dinner, and possibly tomorrow's breakfast as well, for now they were hissing and spluttering and snapping at the edge of the bank, but Eliza and Lavender were safe.

They caught their breath, and then threw it, and then caught it again, and wiped the weeds, slime, and frogs off their faces.

"We got out," said Eliza. But as she said those words she heard an enormous SPLASH, as if some huge and heavy object had just dropped from a great height, into the moat.

Which it had. For, in the middle of the moat, something was thrashing wildly in the water. And two pale white arms were flailing in the air.

"Bonnet?" said Lavender.

"I've—come—come—to—to—to . . ." Bonnet gasped just before his head, and his bonnet, disappeared under the water.

"Bonnet!" Lavender screamed.

He bobbed up again.

". . . to save you!"

He bobbed down again. As his head disappeared under the surface, Eliza realized that the snorting, snuffling, snapping moat-dragons were no longer swarming in the water at her feet. They had all suddenly slipped away.

"Oh no. No! No, no, no. I'm not going back!" said Eliza. But what choice did she really have? They had to save the little giant or they'd never forgive themselves. They'd never be able to forget the sound of his terrified struggle, at least not until they were really old and could no longer remember each other's names, or what jelly was.

"We're coming!" they yelled as they dived straight back into the moat, back through the slime, back through thick weeds like witch's hair, and back toward the moat-dragons, which were now circling around Bonnet as he flailed and struggled in the water.

"Quick!" Eliza shouted. "One. Two. Three . . ."

The two sisters took two huge gulps of air, and then dived down into the stinking green water. And Lavender, her eyes shut tight, reached out below her, and touched something slimy.

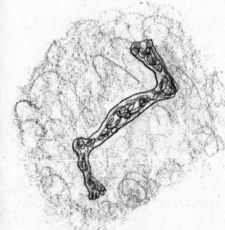

And Eliza, plunging down-ward, accidentally caught hold of the gnarled old leg . . .

. . . of a piano . . .

. . . tuner.

And they kept swimming down and down . . . until they grabbed on to Bonnet's ankles. But a fierce moat-dragon had already grabbed Bonnet by his bonnet.

Eliza and Lavender tugged upward, as the dragon yanked downward.

"GHHHHRR!" went Eliza.

"GHGHHGH!" went Lavender.

". . ." went the moat-dragon. (He wasn't wasting energy making noise. He was concentrating on getting his dinner.)

And he dragged Bonnet and Lavender and Eliza down, and down, and down, as the water got even darker and murkier . . .

Soon Lavender and Eliza had completely run out of air, and they felt so dizzy that they didn't even know which way was up. They gave one final tug, just as the dragon gave one final yank, and tore Bonnet's bonnet off, and Bonnet, Lavender, and Eliza all went shooting up to the surface.

"Gurghhh!" Bonnet burbled, before promptly fainting.

So while the moat-dragon tore Bonnet's bonnet to shreds—Bonnet had never washed it, so it was extremely greasy and delicious—Eliza and Lavender dragged the unconscious Bonnet to the edge of the moat. When they finally reached the edge, Eliza jumped out, and she helped pull out Bonnet and then Lavender, all of them blinking, and coughing, and spitting out mouthfuls of green moat water. Which, frankly, you shouldn't really call water, as it was made of weeds, algae, toads, old newspapers, shoes, hair-oil, broken plates, furniture, and various liquids that come out of dragons.

As Eliza pulled a small snail out of her left nostril, Lavender turned to Bonnet.

"Bonnet, you saved me!" Lavender said.

"Um, really?" said Eliza. She was trying to raise an eyebrow, but no one noticed, because she still had weeds all over her face.

"You came to rescue me!" said Lavender again. "You're my hero!"

"Lavender, can we go now, please?" said Eliza.

But Lavender wasn't listening. She was gazing happily at Bonnet, and saying things that no one had ever said to him before.

Things like: "You're so brave!" and "Onomatopoeia."

"Lavender, we really need to GO. Now," said Eliza.

". . . and you just jumped in and—ooh!" Lavender stopped. "You've got a tiny moat-dragon in your hair—look!"

It was true. Clinging to a clump of weeds on Bonnet's head was a baby moat-dragon, no bigger than a thumb.

"LAVENDER!" said Eliza.

"What a sweet little moat-dragon!" said Lavender. "He's so tiny! I could keep him as a pet. What shall I call him? I could call him Moaty. Or Moatred. Or Moatle. Or maybe it's a she. What do you think, Bonnet?"

Bonnet mumbled something indistinct. He was still reeling from all the nice things that Lavender had said, and he wasn't capable of together a sentence stringing all at, no, no wasn't he no.

"LAVENDER," said Eliza again.

"Or Moataria?" said Lavender.

"LAVENDER!"

"Or Moatvis? Did I say that already?"

"LAVENDER!!!!"

"What?" said Lavender.

As Lavender looked at her sister, she noticed that Eliza was looking very pale, and trembling. And that, oddly enough, Lavender was now standing in a shadow. Which was strange, because it was really quite sunny, and . . . Lavender turned around. And saw what Eliza was staring at. It was another moat-dragon. It was just like the teeny-tiny moat-dragon in Bonnet's hair. It was also the size of a thumb. IF THAT THUMB BELONGED TO AN INTERGA-LACTIC MONSTER WITH UNUSUALLY LARGE THUMBS.

"Ah," said Bonnet, looking up at the beast that was staring down at them, growling. "I wondered what had happened to Violet." He cleared his throat. "Hello, Violet. Um. Yes. You'll probably be want-ing . . . this. S-s-sorry."

Bonnet stepped forward and, with pale, shaking hands, untangled the baby dragon from his hair be-fore dropping the wriggling creature into the moat. There was a tiny splash, and it swam away and disap-peared.

"Sorry, Violet," Bonnet gulped. "No—harm intended."

He patted his pockets. "Would you like a piece of cake? Or maybe an egg? No?"

Violet stared down at Bonnet, and Lavender, and Eliza, and growled.

"Well, nice to see you," said Bonnet.

"I think we should go now," hissed Eliza.

"Unless there are any princes nearby?" whispered Lavender.

"Lavender. It's time to go," said Eliza in a strained voice.

So Bonnet and Eliza and Lavender started to shuffle backward. As they backed slowly away, Violet continued to stare down at them. What was she thinking? Was she thinking: *These are just poor innocent humans, and why not say live and let live*? Was she deciding whether or not to help them escape by letting them climb up onto her back, and then soaring into the air and flying straight over the forest, back home to Old Tumbledown Farm, where she would leave them safely behind and they would watch her go, with tears in their eyes?

Frankly, no. She was just deciding who to attack first. And the answer that she came up with was: *All three of them at the same time.*

Chapter Twenty-Two

In which it is revealed that Lavender's
singing has unusual powers.

Violet roared, and sent a huge ball of fire toward them, then swiped at them with her enormous claws, and snapped at them with her enormous teeth.

"RUNNNNNN!" shouted Eliza. All three of them ran headlong toward the forest, but it was no use. With one scoop, Violet picked up Eliza and Lavender up in her claws.

This was definitely not part of the plan. Lavender shut her eyes. She froze like an ice cream. "GRRRRR!" said Eliza. She was pummeling Violet as hard as she could with her fists, as she tried to pry herself out of the moat-dragon's grasp, but it was impossible.

"Violet!" shouted Bonnet from the ground. "Over here!!" He jumped and waved to get Violet's attention. He clapped his hands. He did a dance. But Violet was much more interested in the two small girls in her claws.

"I know," gasped Lavender. "I've got it! I'll charm her with a song!"

"Is that a JOKE?" said Eliza, still kicking and punching and whacking Violet as hard as she could, although her attack seemed to be about as effective as pelting a whale with marshmallows.

"Whatever you do, don't sing!" Eliza yelled. "It will just make her more angry!"

But Lavender took no notice. A moment later, Mordmont heard the unfortunate sound, and came running outside, astonished to see that the two princesses were still alive.

He lowered the drawbridge, and soon he was nearly at the dragon's side, staring, amazed, at Violet and at Lavender, who was singing at the top of her voice.

"Ooh, lovely Violet, you've got a lovely face,
You've got such pretty fangs, and what a lovely
  place . . ."

"Stop!" said Eliza. "STOP!!!" Because the more Lavender sang, the more violently Violet shook them from side to side. And now the moat-dragon's head began to sway and clouds of purple steam started pouring out of her ears.

"Ooh, lovely Violet, you've got a lovely smile,
You've got a lovely, very slightly homicidal style.
Ooh, lovely Violet, please please don't eat us for
  your tea
'cause I taste worse than brussels sprouts, and
  she tastes worse than me . . ."

"Lavender, stop—your singing is making her crazy!" Eliza yelled. "It's driving her bonkers! It's sending her over the edge!"

It was true. Dragons have very sensitive hearing. To any human who was listening, Lavender's song would have sounded incredibly painful. But to any dragon, her song sounded incredibly, incredibly, incredibly, incredibly, incredibly, incredibly, incredibly, incredibly, incredibly, incredibly, incredibly painful. All Violet's children had fled from the castle to get away from the terrible sound. But the noise had affected Violet so badly that she didn't even *try* to escape. She just reeled and writhed in pain.

"Ooh, lovely Violet, you've got such lovely hair,
You could be on the cover of Dragony Fair.

Ooh, lovely Violet, you've got such lovely ears,
And oh, what lovely screams, and oh, what
lovely tears . . ."

"Wait! No—don't stop!" said Eliza. "Keep going! This could be our chance to escape! Keep singing! Louder! Higher! She can't cope!"

So Lavender kept singing.

"Ooh, lovely Violet, oh what a lovely smell!
A hint of vintage vomit and some deep-sea snot
as well . . ."

"MORE!" screamed Eliza. "More!"

Violet was flailing around so violently now, it was hard for Lavender to breathe, let alone sing. But still she kept going. As she went up an octave, Violet's violet-colored eyes turned orange. Her tail crashed and thrashed and thumped on the ground. She started to wail.

"Someone should make a perfume and call it
    after you:
Eau du Violent Violet, Fragrance de Poo . . ."

That was it. As Lavender hit a top C, and windows in a nearby century shattered, Violet shut her eyes and keeled over. As she fell to the ground, her claws opened, and Eliza and Lavender went tumbling out onto the grass.

A moment later, they started to run toward the forest, with Bonnet bumbling along behind them. They didn't stop until they reached the trees, where Gertrude was overjoyed to see them.

And if they were worried about Mordmont chasing them, they needn't have been. Because when they looked back, they saw him standing beside Violet with a look of amazement on his face. As they watched, Violet lifted up her head, groaned, shook herself, and got to her feet.

Next to her, Mordmont had begun to dance.

"Violet. Violet, Violet, Violet, I have been such a fool!" he roared. "To think it was here all along. Staring me in the face! My fortune! Right here in this moat! Don't you see?"

It was unclear whether or not Violet *did* see. But still Mordmont carried on, his mustache quivering with excitement.

"It is quite simple. The princesses escape from the castle, completely riddled with the Black Death . . . Then you, Violet, pick them up. And what happens to them? Where are the boils? The bumps? The lumps? Gone! GONE! It's you! You, Violet, are a miracle, a medicinal dragon! With one touch you cured those pestilent princesses! Which means each little dragon in this moat is worth a small fortune! All I have to do is sell them at the market, and there we go—a fortune for me! Who needs princesses?"

And because Mordmont was so wildly excited by

the vision of his vast fortune, and his new collection of silver, gold, and platinum trousers, he did not notice the low growls coming from the dragon beside him.

"Now," he said, bending over the moat, "where are they all? Come my little Violy Violettas! Come to Mordy-Wordy! Come on, come—urgh!"

Mordmont yelped and blinked. It seemed that the moat was rushing away from him. Wait! . . . No. It was *he* that was rushing away, up into the air. He craned his neck around, to see that Violet had picked him up by the loop of his dressing gown, and was now dangling him over the moat.

"Violet. Stop that!"

She began to swing him back and forth.

Swish. Swish.

With every swing, Mordmont became paler and paler.

"That's enough now, Violet. Put me down, there's a good dragon."

His gold shoes fell off into the water.

Kasplosh!

"Come on now, Violet! I was joking! Joking! Of course, I would never do anything to harm you or—"

WHOOSPLUSH!

Mordmont never got to finish his sentence, as his dragon dunked him in the moat.

KASPLISH!

She did it again.

Then she took off into the air, flew up over the castle, and dropped him into the moat from a great height.

And, as she flew past the castle, Violet gave it a resounding thump with her tail, which sent the entire building tumbling into the water.

BOOM!

Lavender, Eliza, and Bonnet stood on the edge of the forest and stared, openmouthed, until Bonnet cleared his throat. "Well, bye, then," he said quietly. "I suppose you'd best be going home."

"Bye, then," said Eliza.

"Bye," said Lavender. "You were so brave, Bonnet," she added. "Thank you."

She planted a kiss on Bonnet's cheek.

"So, where are you going now?" said Lavender.

"Oh, I've made a plan," said Bonnet.

"And what's your plan?"

"I thought I might just sit under that tree for a bit," said Bonnet.

"Hmmmn," said Lavender. She wasn't sure if that was really such a great plan. "Which tree?"

"That one over there," said Bonnet.

I could describe it to you, but really there was nothing remarkable about it. It was just your standard tree: branches, a trunk, leaves, that sort of thing.*

"Well," said Eliza. "Do you want to come with us instead?"

Bonnet hesitated. Of course, he wanted to say "YES PLEASE, I WOULD LOVE TO DO THAT, more than I love sunshine and velvet and cheese and jumping up and down." But he was a bit shy. So he just said, "Um, yeah, all right."

---

*Actually, it was Sidney's cousin, Dave.

Chapter Twenty-Three

In which Grandma Maud is suspicious.

Several hours, thirty-two dandelions, three wrong turnings, one asthma attack, five arguments, fourteen owls, two hundred and thirty-two songs, twenty-eight burst owl eardrums, thirty-one huffs, seventy-four puffs, four calling birds, three French hens, two turtle doves, and countless pained looks on the face of Gertrude later, Eliza, Lavender, Gertrude, and Bonnet arrived back at Old Tumbledown Farm.

"Get away, get away, you horrible little man!" said Grandma Maud, who couldn't see very well in the dark and thought Bonnet was Old Mr. Nettles, trying to sell her nettles again. But when she realized that her grandchildren had returned, she was over-whelmed. "My grandchildren!" she said. "I don't suppose you picked up any milk on the way home, did you?"

Then she welcomed Eliza and Lavender with open arms, and welcomed Gertrude with an open bottle of brandy, and welcomed Bonnet with an open look of suspicion and hostility.

"This is Bonnet, Grandma," said Eliza.

"He's our friend," Lavender added. "He's a giant."

"Oh, I'm sure he is," said Grandma Maud, look-ing Bonnet up and down and not sounding sure at all. Then they all sat by the fire, and Eliza and Lav-ender told Grandma Maud the whole story.

"Well," said Grandma Maud when they had

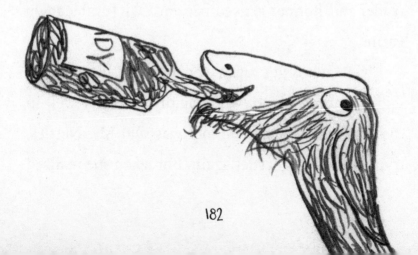

reached the end. "I must say, I was sure you had been taken by the Black Death."

"No," said Eliza.

"Or the Fatal Hiccups."

"Nope."

"Or the Shrinking Lurgy."

"Nope."

"Or Spontaneous Combustion."

"No . . ."

"Or Unexpectedly Lethal Itchy Leg."

"No . . ."

"Or Wandering Teeth."

"No . . ."

"Or Inexplicable Brain Melt."

"No . . ."

"Or Deadly Yellow Bottom."

"No . . ."

"I was so sure it was one of those," said Grandma Maud, sounding only a little disappointed. "But it wasn't to be."

"No," said Eliza. "We're fine."

"For now you are, dear," she replied, patting Eliza's head. "For now."

So everything went back to normal at Old Tumbledown Farm. Gertrude stood in her pen, thinking mysterious thoughts. Eliza cleaned out the pen while Lavender "helped." Except now Bonnet helped out too, with things that he was good at. Like tripping over, and apologizing.

The following night, Lavender and Eliza were tucked up in bed while Grandma Maud read them a story.

". . . And then they all lived happily ever after," she said soothingly, "until they were completely murdered. Well, goodnight then."

"Goodnight," said Lavender and Eliza.

And so Grandma Maud blew out the candle, and shuffled off to bed.

"Night, Lavender," Eliza said sleepily. "It's good to be home." She yawned. Then she curled up, picked a bit of moat weed off her skin, and hugged her knees to her chest.

"My knees!" Eliza said suddenly, sitting straight up in bed.

"What's that?"

"I've got my knees back," Eliza explained. She was quite happy to have them back. From the feel of them, they were a little bit scuffed, but otherwise they seemed to be in good condition. She thought they'd probably gone back on the correct legs too. Although it was hard to be completely sure.

"Nice to have my own knees," Eliza said drowsily, and soon she was drifting off to sleep . . .

. . . and then drifting back awake again, as she heard her sister whispering:

"Goodnight, **Prince Fabian,** Goodnight, *Prince Arjuna . . .*"

"Lavender. Lavender. LAVENDER!" hissed Eliza.

"Mnnnn?" said Lavender innocently.

"Lavender, have you not had enough of princes yet?"

"Oh, was I sleep-talking?"

"No, you were not sleep-talking," Eliza replied

through gritted teeth. She sat up in bed. "You were *talking*-talking. Did all that kidnapping, imprisonment, and escaping from dragons not teach you anything?"

"Of course it did!" said Lavender. "It taught me lots of things. It taught me how spiders are not always your friends. And how sometimes my singing is so beautiful it can make people—or dragons—quite overwhelmed with emotion. Which can be bad for their health—"

"Yes, that's *exactly* what happened," said Eliza.

"And it taught me that if you're going to get rescued by a prince, you should really make sure that he's a true prince."

There was a pause. A pause in which Eliza's face expressed some deeply felt emotions. But, since the room was dark, Lavender couldn't see them.

And so, very quietly, Lavender whispered goodnight to the rest of the princes.

"Goodnight, Prince Rudolph the Unusual.

Goodnight, Prince Chlknklkgkfj the Unpronounceable. Goodnight, Prince Olaf the Simply Fat... Goodnight, Fair Bonnet, who *might* be a prince..." Lavender whispered.

"Goodnight, *who*?" said Eliza, sleepily.

"Hmmmn? Nothing. What? I'm asleep. I'm babbling. Tomato," said Lavender unconvincingly. "Goodnight."

Lavender gazed up at the portrait of Bonnet that had mysteriously appeared on her bedroom wall. Beside her, Eliza was already fast asleep, dreaming of their next adventure.

GOFISH

SARAH COURTAULD

What did you want to be when you grew up?
An explorer, an artist, or a writer.

When did you realize you wanted to be a writer?
I'm not sure, but I loved telling my friends terrifying ghost stories during break time at school. To be honest, some of them are still scarred.

What's your favorite childhood memory?
Sailing across the Baltic Sea, in a smallish boat, and a massive storm. I loved the waves. It was euphoric! I had no sense of danger.

What was your favorite thing about school?
My friends and I had an excellent club where we would make things with FIMO modeling clay. Oh, and I really loved being a rat in the school play of the *Pied Piper of Hamelin*. There might have been forty rats on that stage, but I took it very, very seriously.

What were your hobbies as a kid? What are your hobbies now?
As a kid, I really loved making things with FIMO. Now, bird-watching and going on wildlife trips.

Are you more like Eliza or Lavender in real life?
I'd love to be brave like Eliza. But sadly I'm only like her in that I'm quite stubborn and grumpy. I'm more like Lavender—I spend half my life in a weird fantasy world in my head.

What book is on your nightstand now?
Stone Mattress by Margaret Atwood and *The Secrets of the Wild Wood* by Tonke Dragt.

How did you celebrate publishing your first book?
With fish and chips.

What challenges do you face in the writing process, and how do you overcome them?
Having the concentration span of a baby hamster, an Internet connection, and a love of weird news stories. Haven't quite worked out how to overcome that yet. Oh, and reading almost any book and thinking: "Oh god! This is proper writing! I could never do this!"

If you could live in any fictional world, what would it be?
I'd quite like to live in the world of *The Hitchhiker's Guide to the Galaxy*. As long as I was a fair way away from any Vogons.

Who is your favorite fictional character?
Currently a bit obsessed with Sherlock Holmes. To be honest, I'm pretending this is a literary answer, but it's mainly got to do with Benedict Cumberbatch in *Sherlock*.

What was your favorite book when you were a kid? Do you have a favorite book now?
I really loved *Moonfleet* as a kid—an amazing adventure story with cliff-top chases, smuggling, and diamonds. My

dad read it out to me over a week when I was on holiday and he was in bed with a broken leg, and it was wonderful to listen to. I've got too many books I love now to pick a favorite.

If you could travel in time, where would you go and what would you do?
To an imaginary future where there's less disease, more equality, everyone's solved climate change and they have perfected New York cheesecake.

Although I might stop off at the eighteenth century on the way for a bit of dueling and gambling and tricorne hat shopping first.

What's the best advice you have ever received about writing?
I saw a lecture that Frank Cottrell Boyce gave recently. He talked a lot about the importance of pleasure in writing. And he said that sometimes inspiration doesn't have to come at the beginning. Sometimes you can write something frankly terrible for many, many drafts, and then the inspiration comes in at the end, and breathes life into your writing.

Do you ever get writer's block? What do you do to get back on track?
When I get writer's block, I eat. It doesn't get me back on track. It just gets me to the fridge.

What do you want readers to remember about your books?
I'd like them to remember laughing, hopefully.

If you were a superhero, what would your super-power be?
Mind reading. Creepy, I know. But so helpful as a writer.

What would your readers be most surprised to learn about you?
One of my ancestors was one of the last people in England to be hanged as a witch.

What's the best compliment anyone's ever given you?
I was once chatted up by someone who told me I had "eyes like a shark." It was definitely an unusual compliment. Not effective. But memorable.

What question should we have asked you, but didn't?
Where have you hidden your enormous stash of stolen gold and diamonds?

When Lavender's attempt to become Thumbelina gets them all kidnapped by giants, it's up to Eliza and her amazing goat, Gertrude, to save the day . . . again.

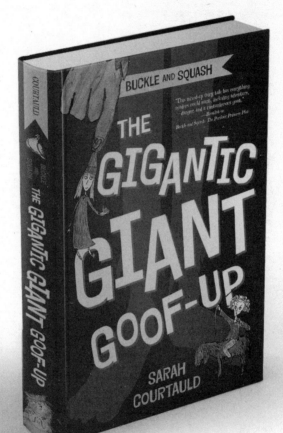

Keep reading for an excerpt.

Chapter One

In which there may be a Vorpel.

"Gurgling Goblins. Venomous Vorpels. Monstrous Murgs," Grandma Maud told Eliza. "It could have been any of them."

They were standing in the yard behind Old Tumbledown Farm. Grandma Maud was scowling as she pointed her stick at a sweater on the clothesline. Well, it used to be a sweater. Now it was more of an oversized flannel. Both its sleeves and most of its body appeared to have been eaten overnight.

"It could have been Gertrude," said Eliza.

"Gertrude?"

"That ate your sweater."

"Nonsense, child!" said Grandma Maud. "That

goat would never touch anything of mine. She's far too fond of me."

Eliza stole a look at Gertrude, their goat, who was sitting nearby. Very nearby. And calmly chewing. As Eliza frowned at her, Gertrude froze.

"I'm sure it was something much more dangerous," Grandma Maud went on. "When it returns, I daresay that will be the end of us."

"Well, not if I have anything to do with it," said Eliza.

She'd been practicing with her new bow and arrow for days. Now she held up her bow, placed the arrow, pulled back the string, shut one eye, aimed at her target—a piece of parchment tacked to a nearby tree—and let the arrow fly.

PEOW!

The arrow soared through the air, toward the tree, past the tree, on a bit, then climbed high into the air, before finally plunging down into the woods beyond the end of the yard. There was an unfortunate squawk.

"I wouldn't bother with your bow and arrow, dear," said Grandma Maud. "If a Vorpel decides to eat us, it will simply eat us."

Hmmmn. If something *did* come to attack the farm, Eliza didn't want to end up as its dinner, or even its predinner snack. There were plenty of man-eating creatures in the forests of Squerb: Diabolical Dragons, Grofulous Ghouls, the Dread Vole of Gweem, the Very Surprising Caterpillar, the Even More Surprising Slice of Ham—and Eliza wasn't going to let them get her or her family. So she spent the rest of the morning practicing with her bow and arrows. Soon the yard was dotted with arrows. There were arrows in barrows.

Dread Vole of Gweem.

Arrows in marrows. Arrows in the nests of worried-looking sparrows. In fact, there was only one place where there *weren't* any arrows—and that was in the target.

Meanwhile, Grandma Maud was reading aloud from one of her favorite books: *Five Hundred Signs That the World Is About to End.* Occasionally, she beckoned Eliza over to read out a particularly frightening entry.

"Venomous Vorpels," Grandma Maud said excitedly, "are highly dangerous creatures that will appear before The End of Time. They can be identified by their long gray tendrils—Quick!" she shrieked. "There! A Vorpel! Fire!"

Eliza looked up. Beyond the hedge at the end of the yard, there *was* a long gray tendril floating in the air. She aimed, fired, and, for the first time that day, hit her target.

Unfortunately, or perhaps fortunately, her target turned out not to be a Venomous Vorpel. Or even a

A Vorpel

Not a Vorpel

Vaguely Villainous Vorpel. It was just Nora, an old lady who lived in the local village, The Middle of Nowhere.

"Morning!" Nora waved cheerfully. She appeared not to have noticed the arrow that was now nestled in her hair. "Are you coming to hear the news?"

"Grandma, should I say something?" asked Eliza under her breath.

"Not at all, that would be most impolite," Grandma Maud murmured. "What news?" she asked more loudly.

"There's a royal announcement happening in the village," said Nora.

"I'll see you there, Nora," said Eliza.

"Royal news," said Grandma Maud, shaking her head. "It's probably nothing important." Then her eyes lit up. "Unless it's The End of the World! Could well be. After all, it *is* written that the world will end on a cloudy day."

"Um, where is that written, Grandma?"

"It is written in a notebook," said Grandma Maud. "A notebook that I just wrote it in."

Personally, Eliza didn't really care about the royal family. It was Eliza's sister, Lavender, who loved that sort of thing. For a moment, Eliza wondered where her sister was. For Lavender was very, very far away . . .

At last, Lavender thought. At last she was where she belonged. Once, she had been just a poor, humble, and incredibly talented young girl who lived with her family on a small farm in The Back of Beyond. But now, finally, Lavender was exactly where she deserved to be. She was standing in a ballroom, gazing into the eyes of her one true love.

"Prince Magnus the Magnetic," she whispered as they began to waltz across the ballroom. In that moment, Lavender felt as if she was floating on air. *He*

dances so elegantly, she thought, *in spite of all the nails, horseshoes, and iron chains stuck to his chest and arms.* As the dance drew to a close, Prince Magnus the Magnetic smiled, leaned toward her, and whispered:

"LAVENDER?! LAVENDER! LAVENDER!!!"

Lavender looked up.

Suddenly, the ballroom vanished, and Lavender found herself back in the yard behind her home. Instead of the fragrance of roses, she could now smell a distinct whiff of mud. And goat. And in front of her, instead of the handsome, smiling face of Prince Magnus the Magnetic, was the frowning, intensely irritating face of her sister, Eliza.

"Lavender, were you daydreaming again?" asked Eliza.

"Er, no," said Lavender.

"Have you washed Gertrude yet?"

"Er, yes," said Lavender.

"Really?" said Eliza. "Because she looked muddy this morning, and she looks even muddier now. Also, were you waltzing with her?"

"Er, no."

"And why is she wearing a crown?"

"Is she?" said Lavender. "I didn't notice. How strange."

Eliza sighed. "Well, do you want to come and hear the Village Crier? Apparently, he has some royal news."

"ROYAL NEWS!" said Lavender. "Why didn't you tell me?"

"I just did," said Eliza.

"Well then, why are you holding us up?"

"I'm not," said Eliza.

"You are! You are holding us up with all this conversation! We should be running, not talking!"

"But you're the one who's talking."

"But you're the one who started it!"

"But does that even matter?"

"NO!"

Then Lavender was off, skipping all the way to the village. While she skipped, she sang. Like many of her songs, this one had many words, and no tune whatsoever.

"A palace is my destiny,
That's where my prince will wait for me.
He'll bring me joy and scones for tea,
Our happiness will spread you see,
Just like jam—or leprosy
(But it won't be quite so itchy).
And we will sing in harmony
In a perfect key
(That's not rusty).
The key of eeeeeeeeeeeeeeee
eeeeeeeeeeeeeeeeeeeee

eeeeeeeeeeeeeeeeeeeeeee

eeeeeeeeeeeeeeeeeeeeeeeeeee!

Because a palace is my destiny."

As Lavender skipped and sang and villagers fled from her, shaking their heads and clutching their ears, Eliza ran along beside her, smiling contentedly. She loved it when her sister sang, because it made her feel proud. Proud of her latest invention: gobbets of candle wax that she put in her ears so she couldn't hear a single note of Lavender's hideous singing.